EMPTY

E M

SUZANNE WEYN

P T Y

SCHOLASTIC INC.

New York Toronto London Auckland
Sydney Mexico City New Delhi Hong Kong

No part of this publication may be reproduced, stored in a retrieval system, or transmitted in any form or by any means, electronic, mechanical, photocopying, recording, or otherwise, without written permission of the publisher. For information regarding permission, write to Scholastic Inc., Attention: Permissions Department, 557 Broadway, New York, NY 10012.

This book was originally published in hardcover by Scholastic Press in 2010.

ISBN 978-0-545-17279-0

12 11 10 9 8 7   13 14 15 16 17/0

Printed in the U.S.A.   40
First paperback printing, January 2012

The text type was set in Alisal.
Book design by Phil Falco

FOR DAVID M. YOUNG, who first brought the issue of dwindling fossil fuels to my attention. Treasured friend, hilarious pal, and brilliant filmmaker — thanks for always being willing to bounce ideas with me.

10 YEARS

FROM NOW

CHAPTER 1

Gwen Jones squeezed out of her bedroom window onto the sizzling roof below. Even through her flip-flops, she could feel the burn of the shingles. The feebly whirring minifan on her night table was no match against the full bake of this night. Whatever relief she could find out here was better than nothing.

Some cosmic cook had slowly started cranking the temperature a week earlier, and Sage Valley was now, at the end of August, blasting at full roar. Wiping sweat from her face, Gwen lifted her gaze to a sagging second level of roof above her, its chipped tiles sparkling under the reflection of the full moon. She guessed that she had more chance of catching a late-night summer draft the higher she went, so she boosted herself over the gutter and inched up, backward and sitting. Kicking off her sliding flip-flops, her bare feet scratched the raspy roof until she was nearly at the peak.

With her knees to her chest, she sat surveying the valley. The ring of dark mountains no longer twinkled with lights from distant houses and stores as they'd done when she was a kid. In the last six months, the price of electricity had gone so high that everyone was cutting back where they could. Most people in town blamed the electricity price hike on the fact that the electric turbines in their area were all powered by oil, and the oil price would not stop rising.

Standing, Gwen peered down over the high hedges just behind her house, to a new housing development. The yard easiest for Gwen to see belonged to the family of a guy from last year's junior class at Sage Valley High, Tom Harris. She could hardly believe they'd both be seniors when school started.

Gwen's pulse quickened as Tom emerged from his house, letting the screen door slam behind him. His appearance always managed to charge Gwen with excitement.

The dark-haired boy threw himself down hard onto the wooden bench of the picnic table in the Harris's backyard, and buried his head in his hands. He sat that way for a long while before resting his head down completely on the table.

Gwen's skin prickled with worry. What had happened to him? Usually, when she saw him out here in the evenings, he was shooting basketball or talking on his cell phone, laughing.

Something was definitely wrong.

Tom and Gwen had been in several of the same classes, but they didn't really know each other. Still . . . she'd been coming up to this rooftop since she was eleven and she had been watching him and his family in their yard at night since they moved in over a year ago. It wasn't as though she was stalking or spying on them. She was up here, and they just happened to be down there. And when they were having one of their family barbecues, it was so nice to watch them. They seemed so normal and wholesome. Not a bit like her own home situation.

Sometimes she imagined herself going out with Tom. Of course she liked his looks — who wouldn't? He could have been a model, with his dark curls and broad shoulders. He played football, and he looked the type, tall and strongly built. But, really, what he looked like was only a small part of it. She liked imagining herself in that warm, cozy family setting, a welcome and natural part of it.

This longing confused her. It wasn't something she would ever admit to. She was more likely to mock it, even. But she had to admit, if only to herself, that part of her would have liked very much to be there.

Tonight, though, she was seeing a different picture. Tom was clearly upset. On an impulse, Gwen left the upper roof and slipped back into her flip-flops she'd left on the lower level. Climbing into her bedroom window, she hurried through the dark kitchen and let the screen door slam behind her.

Outside, Gwen crossed the small yard along the moonlit pathway into the hedges. Squeezing through, she ignored the scratches to her skin as she pushed her way to the chain-link fence separating Tom's perfect world from her very different one.

With her fingers curled into the metal web of the fence, she observed him. Tom's upper back rose and fell in a measured rhythm that looked like sleep. She'd come with the idea that they would talk like friends, but now she wondered why she thought she could help him. She could barely hang on herself.

She wanted to call to him — to ask what was wrong — but then he'd know she'd been watching him. He might not like that she'd seen him so vulnerable. Guys could be that way. She knew it from watching her older brother, Luke, fly into a rage if she ever suggested he was anything but steely and unemotional.

Almost as though he sensed her presence, Tom lifted his head. His red-rimmed eyes were swollen.

Gwen backed away slowly, once again forcing the scratching hedges to part and let her through. There was nothing she could do.

Heading back toward the old, wooden house with its warped structure and blistered paint, Gwen saw that the kitchen's too-bright overhead light had been turned on. Luke was there, pacing rapidly, talking on his cell phone. Gwen's shoulders tightened. Something in his movements told her he was in one of his states.

She paused several feet from the back door, and considered scrambling up to the low roof behind the house and getting into her bedroom that way, avoiding Luke altogether. When he was like this, he always picked a fight, and she was in no mood to fight with him.

On the other hand, why should she have to duck her own brother? She resented it. *I'm not hiding from him*, she decided defiantly.

Luke was turned toward the wall, talking. Maybe she could slip past him. But he clicked off his call and turned toward her the moment she stepped into the kitchen. "Where've *you* been?" he shouted, scrutinizing her with sharp, dark eyes.

Warily, Gwen assessed the situation. Luke wasn't slurring or weaving. That was a good sign. His eyes didn't seem bloodshot, either — also a positive. Ever since Leila had skipped out on them — they never referred to their mother as anything but Leila — back in Gwen's freshman year of high school, she'd been dependent on Luke, who'd been a senior back then. He made the money, though what he did to earn it, she never really knew, and was glad not to know.

"I went to Paris, but I just now flew back on my jet," Gwen snapped at Luke.

"That's hysterical," he grunted sarcastically.

Due to the rising price of gasoline, a flight from New York to Paris cost thousands of dollars. And right now, if things kept going the way they were going, they wouldn't be able to afford the amount of gas it took to get to school. For them, Paris was as far away as the moon.

"If you're going to go out," Luke said, "turn off your fan. And your lights."

Everything counted. That was what they were learning. No matter how small, everything counted.

"I'm sorry," Gwen said. But really, the only thing she was sorry about was that she was alive in this place, at this time. And that even when she wanted to say something that might somehow make things better, she never knew how.

CHAPTER 2

Two weeks later, Tom Harris stood in his driveway staring into the engine of his dad's Ford pickup and tried to remember the last time it had been turned on. He knew for certain that it hadn't been run all summer.

The hoses looked all right. Maybe he just needed to clean the jets and replace the filter. He hoped the problem wasn't the catalytic converter. He didn't know how to fix that himself and, if he had to bring it in, the repair would cost more money than he had.

Carlos Hernandez strolled over from across the street. "Hey, buddy. How you be?"

Tom shrugged. "This thing starts, but it conks out on me and I can't figure out why."

Carlos let out a low whistle. "You don't want that happening while you're on the highway." He leaned in and jiggled the battery cables. "Could you be shorting out here?"

"It's possible, I guess," Tom allowed, bending forward for a closer look.

"I'm surprised it's running at all," Carlos remarked, looking the brown truck up and down. "You don't see gas guzzlers like these anymore. Why not turn this in for a hybrid or an electric?"

"It was my dad's. Besides, we don't have money for a new car," Tom replied. "I hear there's a guy downtown who will convert an old engine like this and make it more fuel efficient. I think his name is Artie. He does it in a garage behind Ghost Motorcycle, I think."

"The place where all those bikers hang out?"

"Yep."

"How much does *that* cost?" Carlos asked, his rolling eyes implying that it would be expensive.

Tom shrugged. "Who knows? But at twenty bucks a gallon, it might be worth it."

"And the price is getting higher every day," Carlos added. "It *might* be worth it to have the car refitted. No joke."

"I never can understand why gas prices are so high. Didn't the oil companies get the go-ahead to start drilling in Alaska?"

"Yeah, and they convinced everybody that they had hit the mother lode. Alaska was going to be the new Saudi Arabia. But there wasn't as much oil there as they thought. It's almost run out. Somebody at the top made a bundle, I'm sure."

It had happened quicker than anybody thought it could — country by country, well by well, the oil had started to dry up. It was right in front of everybody's faces, but they pretended it wasn't happening. They still tried to drive everywhere. They still cranked up their heat in winter and air-conditioning in summer. Reserves were depleted. Alaska was drilled. The price went higher and higher. And while rich people — really rich people — could still afford to get places, the crunch got tighter and tighter on everyone else. Tom didn't like to think about it — because there wasn't all that much he could do about it. Except, he guessed, fixing up the truck.

Tom returned his attention to the engine.

"Do you really think you can get this thing to run?" Carlos asked.

"I have to. I'm going to need wheels if I ask out Niki Barton, which is my goal for this year."

"Whoa! Aiming kinda high, aren't you?"

"You think she's out of my league?"

"Maybe."

Tom shoved Carlos just hard enough to make him totter backward a few steps.

"Sorry, man, but she is," Carlos insisted with a smile. "Totally out of your league."

"*I'm* on the football team," Tom defended himself.

"Yeah, but you're just now getting onto varsity. Her last boyfriend was already a varsity quarterback junior year. He's bound to be captain this year."

"So? The guy can play football, big deal."

"Very big," Carlos agreed pointedly.

"Anyway, they broke up," Tom said. "She doesn't see him anymore, so it doesn't matter."

They turned to look at a girl with black, spiky hair slouching down the sidewalk with a tall, gangly boy. Both of them wore baggy khaki shorts. The girl's black T-shirt was ripped along the bottom hem. The boy's hair was shaven except for a strip of electric green down the middle.

"When did she dye her hair black?" Carlos asked in a low voice. "I don't remember it looking like that last year."

Tom cast Carlos a puzzled look. "Do we know her?"

"That's Gwen Jones. She's been in your grade ever since you got here."

Tom studied her as best he could from the corner of his eye. "Oh, yeah. I recognize her now. Did she change her hair or something?"

"I just told you she did!"

Gwen had reached the driveway and glanced up at them. "Hey," Carlos said, acknowledging her with a nod.

"Hey," she mumbled, then ducked her head down as though not wanting to be forced into further conversation.

"That girl is seriously spooky," Carlos said once Gwen was out of earshot. "I heard a rumor that her mother ran off with some guy a few summers ago and left Gwen with her older brother. I also heard that her mother is a drug addict who never comes out of the house, and that's why nobody ever sees her. I don't know which story is actually true."

"What about the father?"

"I don't think anybody ever knew *him*."

"Who's the guy with her?"

"Hector something or other. He's homeschooled, I think."

"Her boyfriend?"

"Yeah. I think so. I mean, they do look like a set, don't they?"

They both stared back into the engine another moment. "I'm going to get a new air filter and see if that helps," Tom concluded.

"Want to go down to Lake Morrisey later? A bunch of us are going to swim. I still have room in my car."

Tom considered it. Niki Barton had a house on the lake. If she was there, he might run into her. He'd get a sense if she might possibly agree to go out with him, before he actually asked her.

He pictured Niki: so slim, but with just the right amount of curves, her straight blond hair swinging around her gracefully athletic shoulders. But there was no guarantee she'd show up, and he didn't want to be around a lot of people right now.

"Naw, I don't think I'll come," he told Carlos.

These days, just getting out of bed and maybe checking out the truck was as much as he could manage. His dad's death had hit him hard, even though he'd known for months that the cancer was winning. "Another time," he added.

Carlos draped his arm across Tom's shoulders. "Okay. Glad to see you up and around again, anyway. You know how really sorry I am, right? Your dad was a great guy."

"He was," Tom agreed. "At least he's not in pain anymore. Thanks for coming to the funeral and all."

"Yeah, of course." Walking backward, Carlos headed toward his house. "I'll go get that air filter with you tomorrow, if you want. And you've got about twenty minutes to change your mind about the lake."

"Okay."

Tom stood a moment gazing absently at the truck's engine. The thing probably wasn't worth fixing. But his dad had said he wanted Tom to have it. The truck and the old sailboat he kept in the storage shed down at the lake—they were the two things that he specifically gave to Tom. The rest went to Tom's mother. It was only the two of them now.

Tom went back to his house through the side door. The TV was on in the family room off the kitchen, and he could see his mother on the couch watching it. Stepping into the room, he looked at the screen.

The president, Jeffrey Waters, was at a podium giving a speech. "What's going on?" Tom asked.

"We're at war, or about to be," his mother replied.

"With who?"

"Venezuela."

"Venezuela?"

"Yeah. Didn't you see the headlines?" Tom's mother said, pointing to the laptop on the coffee table. "Take a look."

U.S. Troops Headed for Venezuela

Long-standing political tensions between the United States and the oil-producing country of Venezuela stretched to the breaking point in the last week.

Venezuela was a founding member of the Organization of the Petroleum Exporting Countries, known as OPEC. When five of OPEC's original eleven members dropped out of the organization, it was due to the fact that oil fields in the Middle East were running dry at an alarming rate. With the advent of horizontal drilling techniques, the Middle East experienced a brief upsurge in production, but it was only a temporary reprieve. Venezuela, once the world's eighth-largest crude oil exporter, became a petroleum kingmaker.

The opening of the Alaskan territory to unregulated drilling allowed world markets to stabilize. However, the recent announcement that these Alaskan fields are reaching—or have already reached—complete depletion has rocked the worldwide stock exchange and driven the price of oil to a record $500 a barrel in recent days. It has also boosted America's consumption of Venezuelan oil from roughly 20 percent to 60 percent over the last year. This rise in imported Venezuelan oil is also due, in part, to the exhaustion of Canadian oil fields and oil sludge found in sandbanks. Up until this year, Canada was the world's second-largest supplier of oil.

In a speech this morning, President Jeffrey Waters called Venezuela's latest bid to raise its oil price to $800 a barrel an act of aggression that amounted to "an attempt at a bloodless takeover of our country" and said he would not let the United States be "held hostage by this price gouging."

To this remark, Venezuelan president Hector Rodriguez replied, "I am simply exercising my country's right within a free market to set its own price. Take our price or go elsewhere."

The irony of this remark was not lost on President Waters, who in his speech recalled that when OPEC was first formed, its purpose was to keep prices of abundant oil from dipping too low. The idea that there was any place left for the United States to go for its oil, he said, "would be laughable, if it weren't so insulting."

The United States and Venezuela remain at a stalemate, with Venezuela threatening a total oil embargo if the United States does not withdraw its forces from the area. An additional condition set by President Rodriguez is that the U.S. must withdraw troops that stand poised to seize oil refineries that supply American companies. He threatened to attack the 149 oil refineries that remain in the United States should there be any aggression against the Venezuelan refineries.

"War is inevitable," international security analyst Wanda Schaffer said in an interview with the *North Country News*. "It is costing us hundreds of billions of dollars to maintain a military presence in South America — primarily because of the cost of fuel. They're not coming back until they have their fuel. At eight hundred dollars a barrel, the United States will not be able to have its armed forces — or anything else."

CHAPTER 3

Niki Barton drew up a light blue cotton blanket from the end of her four-poster bed until it reached the bottom of her shorts. The blasting air-conditioning was covering her arms with goose bumps. Once the blanket was in place, she tapped the edge of Brock's photo with the tips of her manicured nails. There had to be a way to make him see how wrong he'd been to break up with her this past June. All she needed to do was come up with a strategy.

Brock had gone with his family to their summer home in North Carolina, but she'd heard he was back. He had to have missed her — they'd been going together since the eighth grade.

Niki inspected Brock's strong, attractive features in the photo. It had been taken at the bonfire at the end of September last year. She'd gone there with Brock for the last two years. She couldn't imagine being there with anyone else. And going alone was *not* an option — what if Brock showed up with some new girl, and she was there by herself? Nuh-uh, no way! She wasn't going to let herself get into *that* situation.

But who should she go with?

Tossing off the blanket, Niki crossed to the picture window that looked out onto Lake Morrisey. A motorboat pulled a water-skier along.

A sailfish with a single sail and one passenger moved steadily on the light breeze, making sure to steer clear of the speedboat's wake. Speedboats were really rare now. You had to be pretty rich to have a speedboat. Or a summer house that required a long drive.

The Bartons would leave their lake house here in Marietta tomorrow, to return to their all-year home in Sage Valley. Niki knew it probably seemed funny to some people that they had a vacation home only one town away from where they lived, but the two communities were so different that she felt as if much more than the mere five miles separated them. The Marietta lake house also allowed her father, who commuted to his office on Wall Street in New York City, to have some feeling of summer vacation when he came home every night. And they didn't have to drive for all that long to get there.

Gazing down at the public beach off to the right of her family's property, she saw a group of teens laughing and joking their way to the water's edge. She recognized the particular shade of deep purple of the Sage Valley football jersey one of the guys wore.

Niki snapped up her glasses from her dresser and put them on. Now she could see that the jersey was being worn by Carlos Hernandez. She recognized several of the other guys with him. Being on the cheering squad, she pretty much knew all the athletic types from Sage Valley High. These kids were second-stringers, B-team types, but hanging with them would at least break the monotony of late summer at Lake Morrisey.

Pulling off her glasses, Niki found her box of contacts in her top dresser drawer and inserted them with a deft, practiced touch. She was now glad she'd put the straightening iron to her hair that morning, even though she'd been tempted not to bother. Leaning forward, a few swipes with her brush made the silky curtain of blondness shine. Donning polka-dotted canvas skimmers and tightening the neck knot of her white halter blouse, she hurried out of her room.

Stepping out onto the elevated cedar deck facing the lake, Niki hesitated. It would be too awkward if she just ran down to see these kids. She was captain of the cheerleading squad, after all. It wouldn't suit her image at all to come frolicking down like some puppy excited to play with any new company.

With a quick intake of breath, Niki shifted from eagerness to a breezy nonchalance as she descended the steep stairs to the lake. She glanced out over the lake, setting her sights on the far shore. This gave those below a chance to see her without appearing to notice them.

At the bottom of the stairs, Niki feigned interest in a hand-built, wooden kayak supported between two sawhorses, its carved-out hull facedown.

Glancing from the corner of her eye at the raucous group to her right, she attempted to turn the kayak, as if intending to launch it. The activity gave her an excuse to be there, but she suddenly wished she'd found some less strenuous way of looking busy. The kayak wasn't really heavy, but long and awkward to manage.

"Need some help with that?"

Niki looked up at Tom Harris. Before, when she was looking from her room, she hadn't noticed him there with the others. He was on the football team with Brock, though she'd never paid too much attention to him before this. Still, her casual notice had registered him in her mind as a nice guy. Now, she took in his height and athletic build, his thick, longish, dark curls. She noticed for the first time that his hazel eyes had hints of copper in them.

"Oh, hi, Tom. I haven't seen you all summer," Niki said in a breezy tone. "Don't you have a place on the lake?" She was pretty sure she'd noticed him around Lake Morrisey before.

"Naw, not really a place—just a little land with a dock out on the lake."

"I knew I'd seen you around here before," she said. He grinned a little at that; it seemed to please him that she'd noticed. "Is that where you're going now?" she asked.

"No." Tom nodded back toward the classmates he'd arrived with. "Carlos told me some kids were coming down to swim, so I grabbed a ride with them at the last minute."

"Why was it at the last minute?" Niki asked.

"I wasn't going to go with Carlos at first, but my mom was all freaked out about us going to war and I couldn't take listening to her talk about it anymore."

"Oh, I heard about that. Something to do with oil, isn't it?"

"Yeah, supposedly they're going to cut off our supply."

"So? We'll get it from somewhere else," she said, waving her hand to push away the unpleasant subject.

"I'm sure they'll figure something out," Tom assured her. "They always do. Hot out, isn't it?"

"Awful," Niki agreed.

"Feel like driving into town to get some ice cream?" he suggested. "I came in Carlos's car, but I'm sure he'll lend it to me."

"Won't your friends miss you?"

Tom shrugged. "They'll live."

Niki smiled, pleased that he was choosing her over them. "Okay, sure," she said.

Niki licked the hot fudge from her plastic spoon and cut her eyes to Tom, in the driver's seat of Carlos's beat-up hybrid. Tom had a good profile, she decided, and clearly he could afford to pay Carlos back for the use of the car. They'd gotten the ice cream in town and then driven down the long, flat road back for several miles before Niki suggested that Tom pull over to eat his ice cream before it melted.

Suddenly, Tom swore under his breath and slapped the steering wheel.

"What is it?" Niki asked, alarmed.

"We're on empty! I just noticed it."

"There's a gas station just two miles or so ahead," Niki remembered.

"Good," Tom said, looking relieved. "These cars always have a few miles in them once the gauge reads empty. I wish I'd noticed how long we were riding on empty, though."

"We'll get there," Niki predicted.

"You're an optimist."

"I don't believe in worrying, if that's what you mean."

"*I* believe in Murphy's Law — whatever can go wrong, will go wrong."

"Well, in a couple of miles we'll find out who's right."

Tom chuckled darkly. "I hope *you're* right. I'm not in the mood for a hike in this heat."

Niki grinned triumphantly when the Shell station came into view. "There it is! I told you!" Her smile faded as she noticed the scowl forming on Tom's face. "What is it?"

"Twenty-nine fifty a gallon for regular? Are they kidding?"

"Is that a lot?" Niki asked. "I don't pay much attention to gas prices."

"Yeah, that's a lot," Tom told her as he pulled up to the station. "But I can afford one gallon, enough to get us back to the beach."

Tom pulled up to the gas station entry, but it was blocked by a saw-horse displaying a sign handwritten on white oak tag, attached with duct tape:

OUT OF GAS!!!

"That's crazy!" Niki cried. "How can a gas station be out of *gas*?"

"I don't know," Tom replied. "Are there any more stations down the road?"

With a sigh, Niki considered the question. "I'm not sure. There's got to be other stations if we go back to town."

"It would be closer to try to get to the beach," Tom pointed out.

"Maybe," Niki hedged.

Tom turned the key again as the car's engine sputtered and whined. With a final gasp, it conked out. He pumped the gas pedal hard. The car made a cranking sound as if desperate to come alive. And then, again, nothing.

"I can't believe this!" Tom shouted, sitting back hard against the seat.

"Where's your phone?" Niki asked. "I forgot mine."

Tom took his thumb-sized phone from his shorts back pocket. A holographic message floated in the air: *Refuel battery*.

"I guess we walk," Tom said.

Niki stared down the stretch of unpopulated country road — trees on the left and nothing but tall grasses on the right side. Gaseous heat waves undulated at the level of the asphalt.

"Hopefully someone will come along to give us a lift," Tom said as they set out on the road.

"Or murder us."

"Hey—I thought you were the optimist!" he said.

He was starting to annoy her.

They'd walked for five minutes when a spot appeared on the horizon. As it got closer, she detected an ever-increasing mosquito-like drone.

A motorcycle was racing toward them very fast.

As it came ever closer, Niki could see the driver. He wore a helmet, jeans, heavy black boots, and a vest with cutoff sleeves that revealed two arms loaded with bright tattoos. Someone smaller was seated behind him.

Tom waved his arms to hail them, but the motorcycle whizzed past, kicking a cloud of road dust into their faces.

"Are you nuts?" Niki asked, coughing. "Did you see that guy? We don't want to have anything to do with him."

"Too late now," Tom said, squinting down the road.

Niki turned, following Tom's gaze. She sucked in a sharp, worried breath. The motorcycle was executing a U-turn, and coming right back at them.

CHAPTER 4

Luke idled to a stop alongside Tom and Niki. Staying seated on the back of her brother's motorcycle, Gwen pulled off her helmet and looked at them.

Why was Tom wasting his time with a phony like Niki Barton? It made sense, in a way—he was a jock and she was the cheerleading queen. Still . . . didn't she already have a megajock boyfriend?

Gwen didn't bother greeting them. There was not a flicker of recognition in Niki's eyes, and she couldn't tell if Tom realized they went to the same school. She might as well spare them all the awkwardness and cut to the chase. "Did your car break down or something?" she asked, speaking right to Tom.

"Out of gas," he reported.

Luke snorted with laughter from beneath his helmet.

"Why is that funny?" Tom asked Gwen.

"*Everyone's* out of gas," Gwen told him.

"Why?"

Luke took off his helmet, revealing a thin, angular face. "The stations are hoarding, man," he said.

"What do you mean?" Niki asked, in a tone bordering on irritation.

Luke shot Niki a disdainful glance.

"They want to hold it back to sell at a higher price," Gwen said. Luke had explained all this to her. "They figure we're all going to get pretty desperate. And they're not sure when the next shipments are going to come in."

"That's *terrible*," Niki remarked, in the same tone Gwen imagined she would use if she discovered that a sweater didn't come in the color she'd wanted.

"Mmm, it is," Luke agreed with mockery in his voice. "Super terrible."

Niki glared at him.

"But I can get you gas," Luke added.

"Great," Tom said, brightening. "Do you know someone?"

"You could say that. It'll cost you, though."

Tom's smile faded. "How much?"

"Forty a gallon, one gallon minimum," Luke told him.

"Forty a gallon!" Niki echoed, outraged.

"I only have thirty," Tom told him.

"Too bad," Luke said.

"I have ten more," Gwen offered, digging in her back pocket to pull out two five-dollar bills.

"Thanks," Tom said, taking the fives from Gwen. "I'll pay you back."

Had Tom noticed her eyes flash at his words? Gwen had felt that inadvertent spark of excitement and was embarrassed. If he paid her back, he'd have to come looking for her. They'd talk again.

Plus, he now officially knew she was alive.

Not that it mattered. They were way too different for there ever to be anything—even a friendship—between them. It didn't make sense, this strange attraction she felt. Tom was not her type.

"Where do you live?" he asked her now.

A red flag went up inside Gwen—she didn't want him coming there.

"You can catch me in school," she offered.

"Okay."

He didn't ask *what* school, so he *was* aware of her, at least a little.

"Gwen, you want to wait here while I take this guy to get the gas?" Luke asked.

Not really, Gwen thought, and from the look on Niki's face, it was clear the other girl was equally horrified at the idea of spending time stranded with Gwen. There was no choice, though, but to get off the motorcycle and hand Tom her helmet.

In minutes, Luke was carrying Tom away down the road.

"Where's he getting the gas?" Niki asked.

"I don't know," Gwen replied. Which was mostly true. Gwen wasn't exactly sure. He was probably in touch with someone who had access to this hoarded gasoline—or, just as likely, one of his pals had broken into a closed-down gas station and stolen some.

Luke knew people who sold all sorts of things that had become hard to come by as more shipping and manufacturing had stopped—everything from car parts to cigarettes. Luke also seemed to have some kind of inside track on other hard-to-get items. Gwen had never realized how many things were made from oil. Ballpoint pens had become a luxury because they were made from plastic! Everyone used pencils now. Little kids couldn't get balloons or crayons. Girls in school were hoarding lipstick, shampoo, and even toothpaste—all made from oil-based products. And even if they could get these things, the prices had skyrocketed.

"You're wearing nail polish," Niki said, looking down at the chipped, black polish on Gwen's fingers.

"Yeah." Gwen sat down on the side of the road as Niki continued to stand. What was there, really, to say? She didn't want Niki to know how many things her brother could get her.

Gwen slapped a mosquito.

Niki examined her manicure, rubbing a bit of white polish that had chipped. Her eyes darted to Gwen's black-painted nails. "Sage Valley Nails closed down, you know. They couldn't get supplies. I'm going to have to peel all this off if I can't find any nail polish remover in the stores. And there's none around anywhere. Your manicure looks fresh. Do you have polish or remover? Where'd you get it? Nobody's been able to find any for weeks. I'd be glad to buy some from you. I don't care what it costs."

Gwen had some. Luke had come in with a bag of the stuff one night and tossed the bottle of black and some remover onto the couch beside her. He'd been in a good mood that night.

Gwen studied Niki for a brief moment, deciding what to do — and then she shook her head and said, "No." She didn't want every girl in school seeking her out for nail care products and every other line of cosmetic. In fact, she decided to take the stuff off as soon as she got home. It would mark her as someone with access to black market items, and that was the last thing she needed.

"Then where'd you get that?" Niki pressed.

"A friend." Gwen evaded the question. "It was the last she had."

"Sure," Niki replied sulkily. "What friend?"

"You don't know her." Gwen hoped Niki wouldn't insist on getting the name of this friend, and she didn't. It was obvious from her scornful expression that she realized Gwen was lying to her.

A few more awkward moments passed.

"How long have you been seeing Tom?" Gwen dared to ask.

"I'm not *seeing* him," Niki answered. "We just went for ice cream."

"So you're just hanging out for today?"

"I suppose." With the right side of her lip quirking up slightly, Niki shot Gwen a look that asked, *What's it to you?*

Gwen looked away. "Oh." *Good.* She understood Niki's confusion. Why *should* it matter to her? But still . . . for some reason . . . it did.

That night, Gwen came into the house behind Luke. Two steps in, she stumbled on a box of motorcycle parts in the living room. "Ow!" she shouted. "Put on a light, will you!"

Luke struck a match. His illuminated face seemed to hang there in the blackness. "Can't," he said as his expression once more disappeared into the dark. "Price of electric went up again, and I couldn't make it this month."

"They shut it off?" Gwen asked, her voice rising.

"Looks that way. Our bill was nine hundred dollars for last month, so I couldn't pay it. I don't know what's going on. I never thought I'd wish I lived next to a nuclear generator. But no. We live in a place where they generate electricity from oil-burning turbines. Lucky us!"

Gwen had heard this complaint plenty of times before.

"Yeah, lucky us," she muttered. Then she went back outside. The constellation of Cancer the Crab hung brilliantly, perfectly defined above her. In the next second, she realized why the stars were so bright. Everything in her immediate area was black—all the lights were out.

Gwen ran around the back of the house and got onto the low roof. The sun had been down for hours, so it was no longer blistering hot. From there, she climbed to the peak of the second, higher roof. Looking down, she saw that Sage Valley was completely black. It was a long way off before she could see a patch of lights from some other town once again. Surely *all* these people hadn't left their bills unpaid?

No, this was a blackout.

Just below, Tom's yard was so deeply entrenched in darkness that she couldn't see anything. The next second, a flashlight snapped on, throwing a pool of light. Tom stood at its center. Then, he turned off the flashlight and disappeared.

The impulse to call to him was strong, and Gwen opened her mouth to speak—but then shut it once again. What was the point?

In the intense heat, no breeze stirred. Beads of sweat formed on Gwen's forehead as she sat just below the roof's peak.

She had never known such a deep silence.

There were no engine sounds. No air conditioners hummed. No TV or music blared. The high, ubiquitous whine of electricity on the wire that usually buzzed just below the level of consciousness was missing.

Normally, cars would have been on the road, but tonight she couldn't hear any pass. Was everyone conserving what gas they had left?

In the next moment, the stillness was broken by a rising chorus of crickets. Down on the far side of the road, in front of the house where the creek ran, a loon whooped its crazy call. As if roused by the maniac sound of the strange fowl, bullfrogs initiated a chant of call and response.

Did they do this every night? Gwen had never noticed it this fully before. Opening her eyes, she saw fireflies blinking in the blackness.

"Hey, crazy!" Luke's voice stirred her from her reverie. In the darkness, he stood at the back of the house; she could barely make out his form looking up at her. "What do you see up there?"

"Everything's out for miles," she reported.

"Oh, man!" he yelled, aggravated.

At least we're no worse off than everyone else, Gwen thought.

Moonlight rimmed the peak of the roof, tantalizing Gwen with its shimmer. The last time she'd walked it, she'd been twelve. Why had she stopped? As her body had started to develop, had it become more ungainly—or had she only felt that it had?

Gwen suddenly burned to know if she could still walk the narrow peak. Glancing down, she checked that Luke had gone back inside.

Climbing higher on all fours, she made it to the peak and squatted. Squeezing her abdominal muscles tight, she lifted herself, arms outstretched.

Inhaling deeply, she balanced. Had she tied the shoelaces of her sneakers? Gwen hoped so, because she didn't dare look down for fear of losing her balance.

This was insanity—but it filled her with a serene happiness. She was lifted above the dark world below. Silver moon energy poured into her, traveling from the roof and up her body as she stepped into its light.

She could still do it.

Like riding a bike.

First one foot swung forward, and then the other. Steady on.

Deep, slow breaths.

Gwen was halfway across the roof when a dark form abruptly appeared in her path. Startling, she slipped and began an uncontrolled slide.

A strong hand gripped her wrist, halting her descent.

"Hector!" Gwen shouted, looking up into the narrow face of her neighbor. "Did you want to kill me?!"

"Sorry," he mumbled. "Are you okay? Can I let go now?"

Gwen pulled herself to a sitting position and tried to contain her temper, because she knew it was really more surprise than anger she was feeling. "Why did you come up here?" she repeated.

Hector lived in the trailer home down the road. Gwen had met him while walking to the corner deli one day, and he'd started coming around. She hadn't yet decided if he was just being friendly or if he was looking for a girlfriend.

Hector sat and pulled his knees to his chest. In the dark, his Mohawk made him look almost like an exotic bird. "There's nothing to do. I figured I'd find you up here."

"Next time whistle or say something, would you? Don't just sneak up on me."

"Sorry," Hector repeated. "Don't you think what you were doing was kind of dangerous?"

"Probably. Whatever," Gwen answered with a shrug.

"Why did you do it?" he pressed.

"I like the feeling."

"Don't do it anymore, okay?" Hector said, his words half request, half command.

"Stop worrying. I have good balance. I was on the gymnastics team in my freshman year. I walked the balance beam."

"Why'd you stop?"

"Those gymnastic girls were real cliquish. I didn't fit in. And once they stopped being able to afford the buses, the only team we could ever compete against was Marietta. That got old pretty quick."

"Are you ready for school to start next week?" Hector asked.

"No. You're lucky you don't have to go back."

"Hey—when you're homeschooled, you *never* have school vacation," he reminded her. "So what do you think of all this—I mean the war and the no gas and no light?"

"The war part stinks," Gwen said. "The rest of it isn't so bad. I kind of like the quiet and the dark. Luke and I don't have air-conditioning, anyway, so that doesn't matter to me."

"We don't have it, either," Hector said. "I would like my electric fan to work. I miss TV, too, especially the science fiction channel."

Gwen laughed. "My tablet isn't charged, so I can't even read. Too bad there aren't libraries open anymore; you could go get an actual book. Do they still have real books?"

"I think the old ones are all stored in a vault in Washington, or something."

"I've never seen the stars so bright," Gwen observed. "What do you think is out there, Hector?"

"I don't know. Lots and lots of space, I guess."

"But why is it out there? What does it mean?"

"I suppose there's some larger plan, a bigger picture than we can ever be aware of."

Gwen looked up at his face, its angular arches and planes rimmed with silver light. His dark, expressive eyes filled with moon. Hector could be deep sometimes, Gwen thought. "What good is a bigger picture if we can never know it for sure?" she asked.

Hector shrugged and smiled. "Trying to figure it all out keeps life interesting, I guess."

Little by little, lights blinked on around the valley. "The power's back," Gwen said.

"I don't think so. People are probably getting their small generators going."

"Don't those need electricity?"

Hector shook his head. "Lithium battery chips."

"Better hoard battery chips, then," Gwen commented. "If we can't get them, we'll be in real trouble."

"Whatever happens, at least we have each other," Hector said.

Gwen looked at him sharply. There was something in Hector's low tone of voice, or maybe it was the bend of his body that made her think he was about to lean in for a kiss. "What do you mean by that?" she asked, moving back.

Hector looked hurt. "Mean by what?"

"'We have each other.'"

"What do you think it means?"

"I don't know," Gwen insisted. She had an idea of what it meant on her end of things, but she wasn't completely certain. Friends? More than friends?

"It means I'll be there to help if you need me."

Gwen stood. "Uh, thanks, Hector, but I never need anyone. That's not how I am."

"Someday you might need some help. Everyone does, sometimes," Hector insisted.

"Not me," Gwen said as she sat and began inching quickly down the roof. "I'd better get inside. It's going to take a while to wash my hair by candlelight."

"You're going to wash it in freezing cold water?" Hector asked.

"Why should the water be freezing?" Gwen replied as she made her way down the roof.

"Your furnace has an electric start button. Unless you have a hot water tank—and I doubt you do in a house this old—you don't have any hot water."

"I guess that means sleep," Gwen said. That's what the whole town would do—sleep until things got better. Because there was nothing else they could do.

Bolivia Backs Out of Lithium Trade Talks With U.S.

Vows to Support Venezuela

The fighting in Venezuela, centered just outside the city of Maracay, has been brought to a temporary cease-fire in recent days while U.S. diplomats hold emergency sessions with Bolivian representatives.

Bolivia is the world's greatest supplier of the valuable mineral lithium. When the lithium fields of Bolivia were seized by the People's Revolutionary Party (PRP), party leaders called lithium "the mineral that will lead us to the post-petroleum era." Their insistence on tightly controlling trade and pricing agreements led, in part, to the loss of the hybrid-car initiative in the U.S. that same year, with fuel-efficient cars taking their place. The U.S. failed to make trade agreements with the Chinese to tap into its lithium supply in Tibet, and had to depend exclusively on the much smaller lithium-producing salt flats of Chile and Argentina.

In the eleven years since, the Bolivian PRP has become the ruling party of Bolivia, and new trade agreements with the U.S. and Japan have opened the doors to renewed interest in hybrid vehicle development. As oil grows ever scarcer, the use of battery-powered cars and generators is seen as increasingly crucial. Any stall in talks with Bolivia could have dire consequences for the global economy.

CHAPTER 5

Tom thought that school might be canceled because of all the blackouts and the hard time people were having finding fuel. But the morning of the first day of school, the call Tom had been hoping for hadn't come. Instead, he had to walk the two miles to school — there hadn't been buses for as long as he'd been there — and head back to class. Most kids hadn't been able to charge their tablets, and teachers were being discouraged from using the electric boards, so class was bordering on chaos. Concentrating on what the teachers were saying was harder than ever. Tom found himself praying the school's generator would fail and the lights would suddenly blink out, causing the students to be sent home. Then he realized home wasn't much better.

After a week back, things hadn't really improved. Tom caught up with Carlos as they left their creative journalism English elective. "I thought the English electives were going to be fun, but this is a total bore," he complained.

"I know," Carlos agreed. "This substitute, Mr. Ralph, stinks. Where is Mr. Curtin, anyway? That's the main reason I signed up for the class. Did he quit or something?"

Tom shook his head. "I heard he lives so far away that he can't get enough gas to come to work each day, so he's on temporary leave."

"It was cold last night, did you notice?" Carlos asked as the two of them headed for the cafeteria.

Tom blasted him with laughter. "Did I notice? How could I *not* notice? I begged Mom to turn on the heat, but she couldn't. Our oil tank is nearly empty. The oil company doesn't know when it's going to be able to deliver. Mom has to save what we have in case it freezes. She says if the pipes in the house freeze, they could burst."

"My parents don't have any oil, either. I slept with four blankets," Carlos recounted. "And I wish the electric would come back on. This is starting to drive me nuts."

"Mom has an emergency crank radio. Last night, I heard that they expect emergency oil to bring the electric turbines back up by tomorrow."

"I can't wait," Carlos said. "I've been going to sleep at six o'clock because there's nothing to do. And then I wake up in the middle of the night, and I can't even watch TV. If I could at least recharge my phone, I'd call you and make you crazy, too."

"I already feel crazy. My mother keeps wanting us to spend time talking, and then all she wants to do is freak out about this war. I was actually glad to come back to school this morning, because at least the generator means there's hot water. I actually enjoy showering after gym now."

Tom saw Gwen turn the corner, walking toward them. He'd paid her money back on the first day of school, and ever since then they'd chatted briefly in the hall sometimes. He considered their relationship as being friendly, even if they weren't exactly friends.

Each time they met, Tom had the sensation Gwen was a girl in a costume, that she was hiding under the dark eyeliner, the jet-black hair, and the scruffy outfits. She was entirely different from Niki—and he still thought of Niki as the perfect girl, even though she'd forgotten all about him. Yet he thought Gwen was also attractive, intriguing, and sort of mysterious but with a dry sense of humor. There was something about her that he really liked.

Too bad she was seeing that guy with the Mohawk—the home-schooled one. He'd have asked Gwen if she wanted to hang out with him sometime if she wasn't already involved with another guy.

"Hey, Gwen," he greeted her when she was close. "Why weren't you in journalism?"

Gwen checked to see who else was nearby before replying in a conspiratorial voice, "I ditched. I can't take that Mr. Ralph—what a dork. I wish Curtin would come back."

"We all do," Carlos said. "Did you freeze last night?"

Gwen answered with a little shrug, not meeting his eyes. "Not really."

Tom suddenly realized what she meant. He stepped in closer to her. "Your brother has oil, doesn't he?" he whispered.

Gwen didn't answer, but she didn't have to. Tom could tell that her choppy, black cut was clean. Most of the girls at Sage Valley High had taken to wearing their hair pulled back or in braids to hide the fact that it was overdue to be washed. It was just too dark at night and the water was too cold for them to attend to their usual hair routines, at least not with the same care they usually used. The ones who washed it in the school showers didn't have time to style it.

"Where is he getting the oil?" Tom asked in a low voice. "Is it at the same place we went that day I got it from him?"

Tom remembered the old building where Luke had taken him. Luke had parked his motorcycle in front of the burned-out wooden building and insisted Tom stay with it while he disappeared around the back, before returning in ten minutes with a red canister.

"I told you . . . he doesn't have oil. That was just that one day. He can't get it anymore."

"I don't believe you," Carlos challenged her softly. "You can trust us. We won't tell anyone else."

"He *doesn't* have oil or gas or anything," Gwen insisted.

"Then why weren't you cold?" Tom asked.

"It wasn't *that* cold."

"I froze my butt off! You're crazy," Carlos scoffed.

"Could be," Gwen agreed. "You're probably totally right about that."

"Come on, Gwen, tell us," Tom coaxed. "We just want to buy enough to get a generator going. The nights are really getting cold."

Gwen looked at him and their eyes connected. Tom felt something pass between them before they both darted self-consciously out of the connection.

"Anyway, I have to go to the computer room," Gwen said, backing away down the hall.

"It's closed," Tom told her.

"They hook into the generator between one and two," Gwen called over her shoulder.

Tom waved good-bye as he watched her disappear into the crowd.

"What do you think of her?" Carlos asked.

"She's interesting," Tom replied. "She has sad eyes."

"I like her stuff when she reads it in journalism. She's a good writer. Smart," Carlos said. "She might be pretty if she wasn't so weird."

"Yeah," Tom agreed. She *was* pretty. Not his type, of course, but still . . . there was that something about her.

Tom and Carlos arrived at the wide double cafeteria doors and instantly saw the sign taped to it: CLOSED UNTIL FURTHER NOTICE. Mr. Ralph was nearby, and Tom turned to him. "No cafeteria?" he asked, jerking his thumb toward the sign.

"No refrigeration and no electricity equals no lunch," Mr. Ralph replied without stopping. "It's more than the generator can handle. You can go out to eat if you want. New rule."

"Do you have your car?" Tom asked Carlos.

"Yeah, but I just have enough gas to get home — I hope. I'm cruising on fumes as it is."

"That stinks."

"No luck with your dad's truck?"

Tom shook his head. "Not yet. There's no rush. I couldn't afford to put gas in it even if I got it going."

"Doing anything this weekend?" Carlos asked as they headed down the hall.

"I'm supposed to go clean out the boathouse. Mom wants to sell the boat, so she asked if I would clean out the storage shed that has all the boat stuff in it."

They were nearly to the lobby. "What are we going to eat?" Carlos asked, throwing his arms wide in frustration.

"I don't know!" Tom admitted. "What's everyone else doing?"

"I have no idea." Carlos shook his head. "This is crazy, man. We're stuck here in school with no food and no wheels."

"We can see if someone has a bag lunch we can grub from," Tom suggested.

"Now you're thinking," Carlos agreed. "We'd probably do better if we split up. No one will have enough for both of us."

"You're right. See ya later."

"Later."

Students were milling around the halls and spilling out into the front walkway by the near-empty parking lot. Tom slid his student cash card into the vending machine before noticing every single thing was out. He wandered outside to the front of the building and scanned the parking lot across the road from the front entrance.

A red two-seater sports car pulled in front of him. The window closest to him went down, and Niki leaned across the passenger seat.

After their disastrous ice cream outing, Niki had been avoiding him. Tom could never make eye contact or find an opening to talk to her. He was sure she saw him as a complete loser for getting her stranded like that. And anyway, he'd heard she'd gotten back together with Brock. They were holding hands and nuzzling each other in the hallway once again, just like last year. He'd been delusional to think he ever had a chance with her.

"What are you doing?" Niki asked, looking sleek in her hot pink sweater, her perfect blond hair seemingly unaffected by recent conditions.

"Looking for lunch."

"Want to go to my house? I'll make you a sandwich or something."

Why was she being so nice to him? "Okay," he said. He caught sight of Brock standing in the parking lot with some of the guys from the football team. Easily six-foot-three and every inch the star quarterback,

Brock was a formidable figure, not someone Tom would especially want to anger. "Maybe we shouldn't go."

"Why? Because of Brock? He has nothing to say about it. We broke up."

"Again? Whose idea was that?" Tom asked, noticing when he got closer that she smelled like a heady mixture of lemon and honeysuckle perfume.

Niki hesitated. "Mine."

Tom didn't believe her. But maybe it was only wishful thinking on his part. If Brock broke up with Niki, he shouldn't mind seeing Tom and Niki together.

Deciding to chance it, Tom slid into the passenger seat.

To get out of the school parking lot, they had to drive right past Brock. As they passed, Brock glanced nonchalantly into the car. Tom couldn't read his expression, but he felt relieved that Brock wasn't glaring at him angrily. Just the same, he unintentionally slid lower in his seat.

"So, I haven't seen much of you, Tom," Niki said brightly, as though this wasn't something she had intended. "What have you been up to?"

"Not much. Since I'm not playing football, I've been looking for a job, but so far I haven't been able to find one. Mostly, I've been trying to get my father's old truck up and going."

"Oh, I heard about your father. I'm so sorry. I would have said something last time I saw you, but I didn't know."

"It's okay. Thanks."

Niki turned out of the school lot and drove down a block of neat houses. Glancing to his right, Tom noticed a tall, thin man with a head of thick, blond hair, standing on a lawn. "Pull over a minute, please," Tom said.

"That's Mr. Curtin," Niki noticed, stopping at the curb.

Tom sprang from the car. "Mr. Curtin!" he called, waving. Niki stayed in the car; clearly, she wasn't looking for any student-teacher reunions this afternoon.

The teacher looked to Tom and smiled. "Why aren't you in school, Tom?"

"Why aren't *you*?" Tom inquired. "I'm supposed to be in your journalism elective."

"I'm coming back. I've finally bought this house closer to the school, so I can walk to work. I got a great deal because the former owner is moving south so his heating bill won't be so high. I was just out here looking for a place to dig a root cellar."

"What's that?" Tom asked.

"A big hole in the ground for keeping food; it's naturally cool so I won't need refrigeration for things like potatoes, carrots, yams—root vegetables. I plan to grow my own vegetables next spring."

"Why don't you just go to the grocery store like everybody else?" Tom asked.

"Where do you think that produce comes from?" Mr. Curtin replied.

Tom had never really thought about it. "I don't know. Farms, right?"

"Like all the farms in this town?"

"Are you kidding? There are no farms here anymore."

"Exactly. The food is brought in by trucks and, especially in the winter, on freighters from places like South and Central America. Have you seen the supermarket produce department lately?"

"No, my mom does the shopping."

"Check it out sometime. The fresh produce shelves are just about empty. The price of food in general has more than tripled. You need gasoline for trucks and freighters, and they pass that cost on to consumers like us. I wish I'd grown a garden this summer, but I never expected that things would get this bad this fast."

"Nobody did," Tom said.

A slim, blond woman with her hair in a ponytail approached. "Mary, this is one of my students, Tom Harris. Tom, my wife, Mary," Mr. Curtin introduced them. "Tom and I were just saying how nobody expected everything to fall apart so fast."

"Well, we all should have seen it coming," Mrs. Curtin said. "We've been headed down this road for a while. I guess no one—including me—thought the oil would really run out. We had no idea that everything is made from oil—plastic, insecticides, cosmetics—everything. Shampoo and soap are made of hydrocarbons, linked and processed from oil. Bricks and concrete are made with oil. The shingles on our roof. Carpet. Fertilizer. The asphalt we use to pave our roads—that comes from the bottom of the tank after oil's been refined. When there's no oil, the bottom of the tank is empty."

"My wife has her PhD in bioengineering. She's been very involved with ecological issues for the last ten years," Mr. Curtin explained.

"So I should have known better. People have been predicting this would happen for the last thirty years," Mary Curtin said. "Now, at last, it's happened."

"What's happened, exactly?" Tom asked. "I mean, once this thing with Venezuela is settled, we'll be back to normal, right?"

"Venezuela is bluffing," Mr. Curtin said.

"What do you mean?"

"Their oil supply is running dangerously low. They know it. It's a con game to keep the world from bothering with alternative fuels. Saudi

41

Arabia overreported its oil production for years until its supply of oil was completely gone. In the 1950s, the United States was the largest producer of oil in the world — then it just finally ran out and we became dependent on foreign oil."

"Now the foreign oil is almost gone," Mrs. Curtin added. "It's a non-renewable resource. Our military is fighting for something that's not even there anymore."

"Then why are they doing it?"

"Maybe we want to get in and see if we can find more oil. It could be a move to corner Bolivia. The lithium is what we need if we're going to be using more and more lithium batteries — though lithium will run out eventually, too," Mrs. Curtin explained.

"Still . . . it could tide us over until we come up with something better," Mr. Curtin allowed. "We're trying to gear up nuclear and wind-power facilities — but, ironically, it's hard to build them without oil."

Tom absorbed this news with a sense of growing dread. The subject scared him, and it wasn't a good feeling. He didn't want to talk about it anymore. He glanced back at Niki waiting in the car.

"When are you coming back to school?" Tom asked his teacher.

"Next week."

"Great. Well, I'll see you then."

"See you then."

"Nice to meet you," Mrs. Curtin said with a wave.

"You, too," Tom replied, pulling open his car door.

"What was *that* about?" Niki asked when Tom got back in the car.

Once again, he found her lemon-and-honeysuckle scent drew him to her.

"What did he say?" she prompted.

"Oh, just about how the world is falling apart and there's nothing we can do to stop it," Tom said, trying to sound as if it didn't matter. And when he was there beside her, drinking in her citrus-sweet perfume, it really didn't seem to matter — nothing mattered.

"What else is new?" Niki scoffed. "The world's always been about to collapse. But it never does. Isn't that what social studies is all about?"

"Yeah, I guess."

They drove for a while in silence.

"Didn't we just pass your road?" Tom pointed out.

"Oh, I forgot to tell you — we've moved back into the lake house in Marietta. The electricity stays on all the time in Marietta! It's not like here in Sage Valley, where it blinks on and off and nobody knows when or why. Things are much better in Marietta."

"How is Marietta managing that?" Tom asked, shocked at the news.

"People in Marietta have connections," Niki replied slyly. "There's a rumor that they tapped into the power grid down county, where there's still reliable electric. We have constant heat, hot water, refrigeration — just like always."

"Wow," Tom murmured. He'd never spent much time thinking about what it meant to be wealthy. Now it hit him, in a much bigger way than before, how much of a difference money could make.

They drove into Marietta. Unlike in Sage Valley's downtown section, here people were on the streets, businesses were open. "Are your gas stations open?" Tom asked excitedly.

"One is. A tanker comes every day and refuels it."

"Where does it come from?"

"I have no idea. There it is." Niki pointed to a Shell station on the corner.

Tom let out a low whistle. "Eighty dollars a gallon!" It amazed him that a line of vehicles snaked out of the station and down the road.

"It's not stopping people," Niki commented.

"Not *these* people," Tom said. "It must be nice."

"What must be nice?"

"To be rich."

"It is," Niki told him with a grin.

They got on the long road to the beach where they'd run out of gas, and passed the station that had been closed the last time. It was still shut down.

After a few more miles, they arrived at the lake house. Niki opened the front door with a remote-control key, and Tom followed her in. "Wow, this is a cool place," he said, impressed. He'd never been in such a luxurious home.

"Thanks."

Niki picked up a note from the glass coffee table and read it. "Mom's out with her friends," she reported. "So, good — that means nobody's home." She gazed at Tom boldly. "You know I've always liked you, don't you?"

"No," Tom admitted with a shaky laugh. "I thought you always liked Brock."

"I was always going with Brock, so I could never let you know how I felt."

Tom was struck by the faulty logic of that, but he had no interest in sorting it out — at least not right then. "I've always liked you, too. But I figured you thought I was a loser after we ran out of gas."

Niki waved his comment away. "That could have happened to anybody."

Stepping closer to her, he noticed how anxious he felt. He inhaled to quiet his rising nerves. This morning, he never would have dreamed he'd be alone with Niki Barton. Even an hour ago, it would have seemed impossible.

Niki stepped closer and took his hand. "I need a date for the bonfire," she said. "Want to go with me?"

Was this really happening? "Yeah, sure I would. I'd love to go with you."

"I'm glad. That's great," she said, her face softening. Lifting her hand to caress his cheek, she kissed him on the lips.

If this was a dream, Tom didn't want to know.

He placed his hand on the small of her back and pulled her closer, kissing her passionately on the lips.

Though his stomach growled, he was no longer hungry for anything but her. Let the world fall apart; he didn't care. "When are your parents coming home?" he asked.

"I don't know. Not until later."

Still holding her waist, he kissed her again.

Hundreds Flock to Marietta Township Seeking Gasoline

The well-to-do residents of the usually quiet town of Marietta have seen their sleepy lake vacation community transformed in recent days. News has traveled fast that in these tough times, the town has been able to parlay the clout of its most influential citizens into tangible advantages—most significantly, a daily visit from a tanker containing gasoline.

The Route Six thoroughfare leading into Marietta is clogged for miles as motorists, desperate to obtain a tank of this liquid gold, line up at the local station—all willing to pay from seventy to ninety dollars a gallon, depending on the day in question.

"We're out of gas by ten in the morning," says Pete Patterson, the station's owner. "Folks come with ten-, even twenty-gallon containers. I don't allow them to fill up with extra gas, though. I only permit each driver to fill his or her tank."

"That's so unfair," complained Alice Tucker of Sage Valley. "My tank is smaller than the tanks of some of these gas guzzlers. Why shouldn't I be allowed to buy as much gasoline as they do?"

When asked about the source of this gasoline tanker, Patterson revealed that Shell has released some of its emergency oil reserves to key distributors.

"That's a lie," Mike Kravner, a spokesman for Shell, claimed last night in a widely released response. "We are sending all our oil reserves to the military fighting in Venezuela and to our troops on alert in Bolivia. As much as we respect the hardship on Americans, making oil and its by-product, gasoline, available to our troops is a higher priority. What the Marietta Shell is selling is stolen gasoline. Patterson obviously knows someone with access to our emergency reserves. We are sending a team of investigators to get to the bottom of this."

In the wake of Kravner's comments, the line of cars lined up outside the Shell station more than tripled. Violence ensued in several incidents when cars with low fuel tanks had their engines quit while on line. In one instance, a motorist refused to push his stopped vehicle to the side of the road or even get out. Several waiting on line rammed the stalled car until it careened down an embankment and into Lake Morrisey with the driver still inside. (He was rescued shortly thereafter.)

Police commissioner Jay Parks announced in a press conference yesterday that due to the chaos caused by this situation, only residents who can prove they own property in Marietta will be able to access gasoline from the station. This was met with loud booing. A man was arrested for throwing a rock at Commissioner Parks.

CHAPTER 6

Niki ransacked her top dresser drawer, searching for a box of contact lenses. Her mother always dropped a new box into the drawer when Niki told her she was out. Where was it? Tom was going to come pick her up for the bonfire in less than a half hour. "Mom!" she shouted, leaving her room for the top of the stairway. "Mom! Where is the box of contacts I asked you for?"

Her mother, a petite woman with short blond hair, came to the bottom of the stairs and spoke from there. "BJK-Mart was out," she explained, referring to the large box store with an optometrist where Niki got her lens prescription filled.

"That's crazy!" Niki cried. "Did you call Dr. Philips?"

Her mother nodded. "He's out, too. He says he didn't get his delivery this week. Apparently, the truckers are refusing to come this far north because they can't get enough gas. Wear your glasses."

Niki stared at the blurred form of her mother, speechless. This *wasn't* happening!

"Mom! I can*not* go to the bonfire in glasses!"

"Niki, I don't know what to tell you," her mother replied with a note of helpless frustration. "Lots of people wear glasses. You look cute in your glasses."

Niki threw her arms up. "You have *got* to be kidding!"

"It's not the end of the world!"

"Not for you," Niki shot back. Brock would be there with his new girlfriend. Bad enough she was going to show up with a second-string lineman — now she would be wearing glasses! "Call Dad," Niki said, coming halfway down the stairs. "Maybe he can find some contacts in the city and Dr. Philips can call for them."

"Your father is already on his way home."

Niki's face wrinkled into a bewildered expression. "Why so early?"

"Niki, come down here. I have to talk to you."

Getting to the bottom of the stairs, Niki trailed her mother into the living room. "What's going on?" she asked.

"Dad was laid off a couple of weeks ago," Niki's mother said as she sat on the couch in front of the large, stone fireplace.

It was as though the shocking news had physically hit Niki, leaving her unsteady on her feet. "Are you kidding? Why?"

"This oil and gasoline shortage has affected stock prices around the world. People's stock values are plummeting, so they're pulling their money out of Dad's brokerage in record numbers. Because of this, and the cost of keeping their building going, the company is downsizing. Massively downsizing."

"So we're broke?"

"Not exactly," her mother said, "but all our savings are also invested in stocks, and our stocks — like everyone else's — are not worth as much as they used to be."

"That's what I said," Niki insisted. "We're broke." That's how it sounded to her.

"We could sell this house," her mother suggested.

"If anyone has the money to buy it."

Her mother nodded. "True."

The expression on her mother's face unnerved Niki. It was crossed with uncertainty, and even fear. Niki felt her mother's dread pass to her like a contagious illness. "How did you and Dad let this happen?" she asked.

Her mother defended herself. "It's happening to everyone. Don't worry. Dad went on a job interview today. It looks very hopeful. Now go get ready for the bonfire. Wear something warm. They say the temperature is going to drop tonight, maybe below freezing."

"Below freezing? No way. Besides, I'm not going—not wearing glasses." Crossing her arms, she rubbed the sleeves of her lightweight cashmere sweater. "And, speaking of freezing, it's *freezing* in this house! When are you going to turn the heat on? I thought Marietta was the town with the oil."

A man's voice cut in. "You still have to pay for it." Niki turned to see her father standing at the front door.

"Dad, turn the heat on!" Niki demanded.

Her father trudged forward, and Niki instantly knew he'd been drinking. It wasn't the first time she'd seen him drunk, but this time there was something wild and desperate in his expression that frightened her.

"Did you have a difficult time in the city?" her mother asked cautiously, going toward him.

"Difficult?" he scoffed, slurring the word. "This is my tenth interview in two weeks. It's not *dif-fi-cult* anymore. It gets easier every time."

"Sit down. I'll make you something to eat," Niki's mother nervously offered.

He shooed her off with a flailing swipe of his arm. "No, our baby is cold," her father insisted. "We can't have that. I have to get her some heat!"

There was a frightening madness in his voice. Niki could suddenly hear just how drunk he actually was.

"It's okay, Dad," Niki said, wringing her hands. Her words had set him off. If only she could call them back somehow. "It's not really that cold. I don't mind."

He stumbled toward a button beside the fireplace and hit it. Gas jets ignited into blue tongues of flame around a ceramic log.

"That's better. Thanks," Niki said quickly. "I'm warm now."

"Yes, much better," her mother agreed. "Now let me get you something to eat, George."

"I'm not hungry," her father replied with a rumbling, disdainful laugh. "That flame won't last. Didn't you know? There's hardly any propane left in the gas tank. The price of propane gas has gone through the roof. And you can't get any, anyway. It's all being sent to the war effort."

George Barton lunged forward and grabbed hold of a straight-back chair. Niki jumped back as her father lifted the chair above his head and smashed it hard against the fireplace, sending its pieces flying. "Here's firewood!" he announced as he pulled open the protective glass fire window and tossed in rungs of the shattered chair. "This will burn."

"George! Stop! Please!" her mother pleaded. "That chair was an antique."

"Get used to it, Kate. This is how we're going to be living now. If we can't eat it, we're going to burn it." George Barton pulled a mirror off the wall and banged it onto the fireplace mantel.

"Stop it!" Kate Barton screamed, but her husband ignored her as he yanked the wooden frame from the mirror.

"Fire sale—everything must go!" he cried as he threw the mirror frame into the now roaring fire.

Niki clutched her mother's trembling arm. "He's gone crazy! What should we do?"

Her mother began to cry and covered her wet eyes with one hand. "I don't know," she admitted, her voice quavering, tears brimming. "I don't know."

An hour later, Niki stood as close to the bonfire as she could get. Her mother had been right: The night was unexpectedly frigid for September. In the fire's jumping light, she could see Tom beside her, his face a shifting landscape of shadows. She kept hold of his hand for warmth and also for guidance, since beyond a small circle close by, everything was a blur.

"You okay?" Tom checked.

She smiled tightly and nodded. "It's cold, though."

He shifted her around so she was closer to the fire. "Better?"

"Better," she confirmed.

"You sure you're all right?"

She was still shaken by the scene at her house. When Tom had finally rung her front doorbell, she'd abandoned her mother, leaving her alone to deal with her drunken, raging father. Grabbing Tom's hand, she'd fled down the front walkway into his old wreck of a truck. Normally, she'd have been horrified to be seen in such a piece of junk, but tonight anything that would take her away from her house was a welcome sight.

"Are you upset that I was so late?"

Niki hadn't wanted to talk about what had happened with her father, so she said nothing, tried to act like nothing was wrong. But clearly he could tell she was troubled. "No, I understand that you couldn't find gas. Even in Marietta, you have to know exactly when to show up at the station. And that truck of yours must suck up a ton, too."

"Way too much."

"The smoke is getting to my eyes," Niki offered as a partially true explanation for her strained eyes. She hadn't told him that she'd come out without contacts or glasses. No doubt, her unfocused expression was adding to his sense that something was not right with her.

"Do you want to move away from the fire?" Tom asked.

"No, then I'll be cold." Niki laughed lightly at her dilemma. "I'd rather be warm."

The night had been full of song and a friendly rivalry between some members of the Marietta Mariners football team, Sage Valley's rivals. The next big football game would be a home game with the Mariners. Technically, the bonfire was a Sage Valley event, but every year a group of Mariner players and cheerleaders showed up to taunt and be taunted in return.

Tom wrapped his arm around Niki's shoulder and pulled her tighter. She took in his warmth and the pleasantly smoky smell of his jacket. Maybe he was someone she really could like. She hadn't started out to do anything more than make Brock jealous. But, with her limited vision, she couldn't even find Brock in the crowd. And after the time she'd spent kissing Tom the other day . . . well, Niki was growing to like him more than she'd suspected she would.

From the parking lot, someone hurtled an enraged curse into the night.

A windshield shattered.

"What's happening?" Niki asked Tom.

"I'm not sure," he answered. He let go of her hand. "Stay here. I'll find out."

The crowd around the big fire separated to make room for a bunch of Mariner cheerleaders. To Niki, they were just moving blurs, but she could clearly hear them chanting the Mariner cheers. Around them, her classmates booed and heckled good-naturedly.

Would her cheering squad be expected to respond to this? Did they last year? She hadn't been elected captain then, and couldn't remember if they'd assembled to face off against the Mariner squad. Could she get through a routine half blind? She'd have to insist it wasn't one with a pyramid or any kind of throw and catch.

All of a sudden, Niki became aware of a large person standing beside her, tall and square—she'd know Brock just by the smell of the fabric softener his mother used. "Hey, Niki. Are you here by yourself?" he asked, his voice neutral.

"What do you care?" Niki shot back.

"Don't be like that. We're still friends."

"No, we're not, Brock. You dumped me twice! A friend wouldn't do that."

"Aw, come on, give me a break. You know it wasn't working out. Maybe we won't fight so much if we're friends. I wanted to know if you're alone because I think there's going to be some fighting, and maybe you should get out of here before it starts."

A sharp shout carried up from the parking lot on the cold wind. Just as the Mariner cheerleaders were ending their last lines, everyone turned toward the sound. Its sharp, aggressive hostility lifted it above the joking barbs her classmates were pitching at the rival cheerleaders.

"See what I mean?" Brock said. "You should leave right now. I'm going down to see what's going on."

"Shouldn't you leave, too?" Niki suggested.

"I'll be okay, but you should go."

"No, don't leave me." But it was too late. He'd gone.

"They've siphoned all the gas from our tanks!" someone shouted.

Outraged voices rose up on every side. She didn't even know that word—*siphoned*. Niki could see well enough to take several steps forward along with the crowd around her. "What's happening?" she asked a girl who had come into focus to her right.

"Some of the Mariner players have sucked the gasoline from our cars."

"Are you kidding?" Niki gasped. "How'd they do that?"

"Don't they usually stick a hose into the fuel tank or something like that?" the girl replied before she rushed forward with the rest of the crowd that was running off into the darkness beyond the bonfire.

There was more shouting. Down in the parking lot, motors revved but wouldn't start.

Niki inched her way forward. Most of the shouting was indistinct. She heard thumping and pounding, another crash of broken glass. More curses. Occasionally, she could make out a clear sentence:

"Stop hitting him. Stop! You're going to kill him!"

CHAPTER 7

Gwen stretched out on her couch with a scratchy blue blanket held over her head with one hand, a flashlight held with the other. Propped between her stomach and her knees was a tablet onto which she'd uploaded a book titled *Sustainable Future*. From it, Gwen was poring over an article called "Residential Wind Turbines."

The reading wasn't easy to understand. The article had subtitles such as: *Designing and Carving Wooden Blades*; *Alternator Theory and Design*; *Winding Coils*; *Fitting Magnets into Homebuilt Alternators*; *Governing Systems*; *Yaw and Tail Design and Construction*; *Wiring and Fabrication*; *Construction Details*.

In fact, it seemed pretty much impossible to imagine converting to wind power. And yet, the article said it could be done. It also said that— as an individual—it might be easier to work with solar energy. What intrigued her about wind energy, though, was that Luke had so much old motorcycle junk lying around. Wire and motors and all sorts of metal were piled in the shed behind the house.

Tom and Carlos had been on the right track when they'd suggested that Luke had access to stolen gasoline. But it was only enough to keep their old furnace going at sixty degrees and to fuel a small generator for a few hours in the evening. The rest of the gas Luke sold at high prices.

When Gwen wanted to know why he didn't keep more for their own use, he said, "You like to eat, don't you? We need that money for food. Besides, I have to buy the gas from the black market guy, which means filling a truck with gas just to go get the stuff."

Gwen scrolled down to a subhead titled: *History of the Wind Turbine*. She learned that windmills were used to grind grain in Persia as early as 200 BC. The first electricity-generating wind machine was installed in 1887 in Scotland. In America, by 1908 there were seventy-two wind-propelled electric generators. By the 1930s, windmills for electricity were common on American farms.

Outside, the wind howled. She pictured a wind turbine with its blades spinning, producing enough electricity to light their house.

Gwen switched off the tablet. Maybe it was useless. There was so much she'd need to know before she could think about building a wind turbine and installing it on their roof.

Luke and two of his friends stomped through the front door into the enclosed front porch, laughing raucously, in a tone that told Gwen they'd been drinking. They reeked of gasoline and body odor as they dragged in an array of various plastic containers — juice and milk jugs, large water jugs, and even soda bottles, along with red containers.

Tossing off her blanket, Gwen left the tablet on the couch. Going toward the porch, she recognized the strong odor of gasoline before she even got there. "Did you just come up from the city with that?" she asked Luke.

"None of your business where we got it," Luke told her, though he appeared to be in a good mood. "We're going to make a bundle on this.

People are so desperate, they'll pay anything, especially over in Marietta, where they can afford it."

"Isn't what you're doing illegal?" Gwen asked.

Luke looked to his two friends, a tall, skinny guy in motorcycle leathers named Mark, and a wider, muscular guy with long, black hair who they called Rat. They faced Gwen with serious expressions before bursting into laughter. "Gee, I guess it could be, Gwen," Rat said mockingly through his hilarity. "Are you going to call the cops on us?"

"Of course not, stupid. I just wanted to know."

"You don't have to know anything," Luke said, his laughter subsiding. "Just keep your mouth shut and don't say anything to your friends."

"Don't worry. I don't have any friends."

"What about the boyfriend that you sit around and howl at the moon with? What's his name? Horace?"

"Hector — and he's not my boyfriend."

"Yeah, well. Don't tell him anything about what I do. You haven't already, have you?"

Honestly, Gwen couldn't remember what she'd told Hector. "Hector is cool. He doesn't care what you do. Tom at school knows. Remember, you sold him the gas that day?"

"Well, tell him to keep his mouth shut about it."

"You tell him," Gwen snapped, but then thought better of it. The last thing Tom needed was for Luke to be on his case. "He won't say anything," she added.

"He'd better not."

"Gwen, why aren't you at that thing at the high school?" Rat asked.

"What thing? The bonfire?"

"Yeah."

"That's not for me," she answered dismissively. "I don't really get the whole team spirit thing."

"Yeah?" said Rat. "What's your kind of thing?"

"Helping my brother move illegal gasoline," Gwen replied sourly. "Isn't it obvious?"

"You know what I read?" Rat said. "Oil is the biggest business in the world. Can you believe that? In the world! Do you think all those rich oil guys got so fat by doing everything legally?" He laughed scornfully. "Don't bet on it."

"Don't worry about this being illegal," Luke said, pushing the canisters to the back of the porch to make room for more. "I could make a bundle because I'm willing to take the risk. No guts, no glory."

"Yeah, well, what about me?" Gwen argued.

"You're eating, aren't you?"

"That's not what I mean. What if you get arrested? I land in foster care."

Luke waved her away as he headed back toward the door for more canisters filled with gasoline. "I'm not getting arrested."

"Yeah? Well, I'm not going into a foster home," Gwen insisted. "I'll run away first."

Luke turned at the door and faced her. "Shut your trap and be useful. Pull the blinds and curtains so everyone in town doesn't know our generator is going. Then help us get the rest of this gas."

"Is it safe to store gasoline in here?" Gwen questioned. "I don't think you're supposed to store it in milk containers, either."

"Just get going, would ya?"

Gwen lay supine on her lower roof, staring at the stars. Carrying all those canisters of gasoline onto the front porch had made her muscles ache.

Breathing out, a vapor cloud formed in front of her face. She pulled the zipper of her black sweatshirt up as high as it went. Soon, she'd need some kind of winter jacket. Would Luke sell enough black market gasoline to pay for a new one?

By the time the jacket was an absolute necessity, she might be in foster care. Who would pay for a jacket then? The state? Her foster parents? Anyone?

Would they find her mother?

Thinking about her mother made Gwen's stomach clench with anxiety. She'd run off with her boyfriend when Gwen was in ninth grade. Since she wasn't dead, just missing in action, Gwen and Luke simply hadn't told anyone about it, at least not anyone in charge of anything. Their old house had been inherited from Gwen's grandfather, so they didn't have anything to pay on it. She saw letters that were stamped FINAL NOTICE OF OVERDUE BACK TAXES, but, so far, they'd gotten away with ignoring them.

Gwen didn't even know how to find her mother. She'd simply gone out for a date with Richard and had never returned. She'd left a quick note saying Luke and Gwen were now old enough to take care of themselves. Her job was done. That was how they knew what had happened.

At first, Gwen had been angry. Furious. Enraged by the abandonment. But it was shockingly easy to settle into her new, freer life with

Luke. She could make her own rules, wear what she liked. Not that Leila Jones had ever been strict—Luke always cracked that their mother was "asleep at the wheel." Life with only Luke in charge was complete freedom.

Still . . . did she miss her mother?

A little, mostly when she thought back to when she was small, to a time when her mother didn't drink so heavily and before Richard had brought the harder stuff. There was no sense thinking about it too much, though. Leila had chosen Richard over Luke and Gwen, and that was that.

Luke and Gwen had managed to stay under everyone's radar up until now. It turned out that Leila had quit her bartending job before she left, so no one at work thought it was odd that she didn't come in. Gwen quickly broke off the several friendships she had at school to prevent anyone from nosing around. Doing this made her lonely, and she still felt guilty that she had hurt the feelings of some of her old friends, but it couldn't have been avoided.

So far, no one had even noticed that her mother had split. Gwen did an excellent forgery of her mother's handwriting when a signature was required, not that she thought anyone really checked. If neighbors realized she and Luke were on their own, they weren't getting involved. Her house was close to the development where Tom lived, but that was separated by the hedges. The nearest house on her side was easily an acre away.

Hector was the only one who knew for sure that her mother didn't live with her, but Gwen trusted him. And it helped that he was so off the grid. Who would he even tell?

A twig snapped below the roof, and Gwen was instantly on her knees, peering into the darkness.

"Who's there?" she asked.

"Gwen?"

A dark form appeared from the side of the house, and Gwen recognized it. "Tom?"

Tom stepped closer, into a pool of moonlight, and Gwen gasped. A stream of blood ran from his right nostril. A purple bruise was forming around his left eye. The shoulder seam of his varsity jacket was torn.

Gwen quickly crawled to the edge of the roof and he joined her there. He reeked of smoke and gasoline.

Had he come to see her because he needed help? If so, why her?

"What happened to you?" she asked, impulsively raising her hand to stroke his bruise, then thinking better of it. "You're bleeding."

Tom brushed the red stream from his nose, glancing at his stained hand a moment before wiping it on his jeans. "There was a big fight at the bonfire," he explained, sniffing back blood. "Guys from the Marietta team were stealing gas from our tanks."

Gwen hissed a curse. "Like those kids can't afford to buy it. I thought they had all the fuel in the world over there."

Tom shrugged. "I don't know. But two Marietta guys started whaling on Carlos, so I had to jump in to even the score."

"Good for you."

"Not really," Tom disagreed with bitter laughter. "I was getting the snot kicked out of me. Good thing the cops came when they did. Everyone ran when they showed."

"Want to come inside to clean up?" Gwen offered.

"Maybe later. Is your brother home?"

So he hadn't come to find her, after all.

"Why?" Gwen asked, trying to keep her voice even enough to mask her hurt feelings.

"I walked here from the school. My truck is stuck there; some jerk stole all the gasoline right out of my tank."

"How did you find my house?" Gwen asked.

"A guy at a gas station told me where I could get some black market gas and gave me directions. When he told me I should ask for Luke, I realized I was going to your house." He looked toward the wall of bushes at the back of her small yard. "Hey, you live right behind me."

Gwen grinned. He had only just realized it—and after she'd been watching him from her perch on the roof for so long. "Is that right?" she replied drily. "What do you know?"

Tom missed her sarcasm altogether. "Yeah, we're neighbors. Sort of. If you go behind those trees, you could see right into my yard."

"Huh," she grunted. "That's funny. Imagine that."

"Yeah."

"How much gas did those guys take from you?" Gwen asked.

"I had a nearly full tank, and they took it all. It took me hours to find the gas today, too. And when I did, I had to wait on line for two more hours. I don't even want to tell you how much it cost me. My mom is going to seriously freak out. The last thing we need is this."

"A whole tank of gas jacked right out of your truck," Gwen sympathized sincerely. "Man, that's low!"

"No kidding. So, is Luke around?"

"I'm not sure where Luke is," Gwen told him, trying to dodge the pang of disappointment she felt. For a few minutes there, she had allowed herself to continue to imagine he had come to the house to see her, even though she knew he hadn't. "He went out with his friends a little while ago."

"I don't have any money to pay him right now. But I could get it to him by the end of the week. My windshield got smashed in the fight, and I just want to get the thing home before anything more happens to it."

Luke wasn't inclined to give anything on credit or faith. Gwen sighed, wondering how she could help Tom.

"Do you have a gas container?" she asked.

Tom picked up the red canister he'd set at his feet.

Gwen took it from him. "Wait here." If she poured a little from each of Luke's containers, it would fill Tom's canister and her brother would never miss it.

"Will Luke mind that I can't pay him right away?" Tom asked. "I don't want him to be mad at you."

"If I do this right, you won't have to pay him at all," Gwen said as she pulled the red gas can into her bedroom window behind her. If Luke was going to say the law no longer applied, he was fair game like everyone else.

U.S. Seizes Venezuelan Refineries; American Refineries Bombed in Retaliation

. . . Only 149 American-owned refineries remain in the United States, 26 fewer than existed in the 1990s. Most of these oil refineries are owned by the top ten American oil companies. It is here that oil is pumped from the ground and processed into gasoline.

Although President Waters has decried the bombing of three refineries in the last week, experts speculate that the loss will not significantly hinder the war effort since approximately only 30 percent of America's oil supply comes from these refineries, with the remaining 70 percent of crude oil coming from the Middle East, South America, and Canada. Canada, once the second-leading supplier of oil, has lately reported severe depletions. Canadian tar sands have not yielded the expected supply. There is speculation, too, that Saudi Arabia, Iraq, Iran, Kuwait, the United Arab Emirates (UAE), and, indeed, even Venezuela have been grossly overestimating their supply. Some analysts have suggested that the world may be completely out of oil in the next ten to twenty years.

Junior Senator Thomas Rambling (D-MA) has called for an end to the fighting, stating, "We are fighting over something that does not even exist anymore: oil. The Venezuelans are bluffing. They only want to solidify their position as a world power in the coming reorganization of alliances that will surely follow the realization that the world is out of oil."

CHAPTER 8

Tom and Gwen sat on a dark hill on the far side of the high school's outdoor track and watched the police activity down in the parking lot. The red canister of gasoline sat on the grass between them. Tom leaned forward, watching the police talk to various students. It was difficult to see from this distance exactly which students were still there. Most of them had run when the police had shown up.

"Why don't we just go down and put this gas in your truck?" Gwen said. "You haven't done anything wrong, have you?"

"What if they ask where I got the gasoline?" Tom replied.

"Say you bought it at a station."

"Which one?"

"Any one."

Tom shook his head. "A lot of them are closed. If I pick the wrong one, they'll know I'm lying."

"Hmm."

"See what I mean?" Tom said. "Also . . . they might be looking for me."

Gwen looked up at him sharply. "You? Why?"

"A Marietta guy was about to hit Carlos with a tire iron, and I yanked it out of the guy's hand. When I did, it flew out of my hand and sailed into a window of Mr. Davenport's SUV."

Gwen cringed. "Mr. Davenport, the principal?"

"Yep."

Gwen blew out a low, shrill whistle. "Glad I'm not you."

"Thanks a lot," Tom said, but found his lips twisting into a baleful grin despite the seriousness of his situation. She was a funny girl sometimes, with her wry, bleak view of things. "Nice whistle, by the way," he added.

"Thanks." She flopped down flat with her legs bent. "Are we going to be here all night, do you think?"

"Just wait a little longer and I'll drive you home," Tom suggested. He would have told Gwen that she didn't have to wait there with him, but it was late and angry Marietta kids were still driving around looking to pick fights. It wouldn't be safe for her to walk home alone.

"Who'd you go to the bonfire with?" Gwen asked casually.

"Niki Barton."

Gwen sat up straight again. "Do you really like her?"

"Yeah. Don't you?"

"No," Gwen said, shaking her head and picking at a moon-rimmed blade of grass. "Where is she now?"

"I don't know. I couldn't find her again after the fight. She's not picking up her phone, either. Somebody told me she might have gotten a ride from some Marietta cheerleaders. She's been staying at her lake house over there."

"Oh, how fancy of her! Nice of Niki to stick around to see if you were okay," Gwen quipped sourly.

"It's all right. There was a lot of confusion."

The sound of slamming doors alerted them that the police were getting back into their cars. (There were only three police cars left on the whole squad, so this was clearly a big deal in Sage Valley tonight.) A van probably driven by someone's parent arrived, and the remaining students climbed in.

About thirty parked, empty vehicles remained in the parking lot, nearly half of them with broken windows. "Let's go," Tom said, getting to his feet and lifting the gas-filled canister.

Gwen scrambled up alongside him, and keeping to the darkest parts of the grassy hill, they made their way down toward the truck.

When they got near it, Tom cringed at the gash someone had gouged into the right door.

"At least your side windows are okay," Gwen pointed out, taking in the sight of his smashed windshield.

Tom grunted in·agreement as he opened the small door to his gas tank and began pouring in the fuel. They climbed into the front seats and Tom turned the ignition key.

The engine revved, then sputtered.

Tom swore under his breath.

The second time he tried, the engine roared to life. Tom drove out of his parking space just as a police cruiser turned into the drive to the school. "Say you already had the gas. You don't remember where you got it," Gwen coached.

The patrol car came alongside and Tom rolled down the truck window. The officer got out of his car and shone a flashlight's beam into the truck, forcing Tom to squint against its glare. "Just picking up my dad's truck, Officer," Tom explained.

"Out of the truck, please. License and registration," the officer commanded in a matter-of-fact tone. "You, too, miss. Out of the truck, please."

His heart banging in his chest, Tom stepped down from the driver's seat. Would he be connected to the damage to Principal Davenport's SUV? Did the policeman suspect that he was using stolen gasoline?

Tom took the requested identifications from his wallet and showed them to the police officer, who perused them critically. "Have either of you been drinking or taking any kind of drug this evening?" the officer asked.

"No, sir," Tom replied emphatically.

"No," Gwen mumbled.

The officer stepped closer to Gwen and sniffed. "Why do I smell gasoline on you?"

"I slipped in a puddle of it earlier this evening," Gwen lied quickly. "It's spilled all over the place," she added, gesturing at the oily splotches that now stained the parking lot.

He looked her up and down. "Would you breathe out for me, miss?"

"I told you, I haven't been drinking."

"That's not what I'm checking for," the officer insisted. "Breathe out, please."

Gwen's breath formed a cloud in front of her face and the officer leaned toward it. Then he straightened once more and took a pad from his back pocket. "Name and address, please."

"Rae Gonzalez. 57 Dartmouth Street, Sage Valley," Gwen lied.

"Get back in the truck, please. Wait there."

"You're a fast thinker," Tom commented when he and Gwen were once again in the truck's front seat.

"Well, I wasn't going to tell him the truth, was I?" she replied.

"No. I'm just saying—you're pretty cool under pressure."

"Thanks. Why was he checking my breath, if it wasn't for alcohol?"

"He wanted to know if you'd been sucking up gasoline," Tom told her.

"What?" Gwen asked incredulously.

When Tom had first come down to the parking lot, he realized that some of the Marietta guys were getting the gas out of the tanks using black rubber tubes, which they were sucking air from and then sticking into a fuel tank's opening. The vacuum created by sucking the air from the tube drew the gas out of the fuel tank and into a container. He explained to Gwen how it worked. "It's basic science, like when you draw liquid up in a straw."

"Why would that make my breath smell like gas?" Gwen asked.

"Those guys were using the same tube over and over. After a while, there was so much gas residue in the tubes that they were sucking it in. You should have seen them. They were belching like crazy—sickening gas burps."

Gwen scrunched her face in disgust. "Glad I missed *that*. Someone should have lit a match in front of one of the guys when he burped. That would have scared the snot out of him."

Tom chuckled. "I'd like to see that."

"And this cop thought *I* was sucking up gasoline?"

Tom smiled at her revulsion and shrugged his shoulders. "He smelled gas on you. It makes sense, I guess."

The police officer came back from his car and returned Tom's paperwork to him. "Who worked you over like that, son?"

"I was trying to leave when some guys jumped me. I didn't know them."

"So they were from Marietta?"

"Maybe."

"Did you see who broke any of the windows on your truck and these other vehicles?"

Tom shook his head. "I heard crashing, but I didn't see who was doing it." In truth, he didn't know who had smashed his windshield. He could have given the officer at least five names of Sage Valley guys he saw whaling on Marietta-owned cars and trucks, but he wasn't about to turn in his friends, and he hoped his classmates felt the same, since his name would be among those reported.

In this fight, the Sage Valley kids had stuck together. If it hadn't been for Brock pulling one guy from his back, Tom didn't know what would have happened to him. His injuries would certainly be a lot worse right now. He hoped that sense of camaraderie would last through the police questioning that was sure to follow.

"All right, you can go," the officer said. "But there's a good chance that someone will be coming by your home with further questions."

"No problem, Officer. Thank you," Tom said.

The policeman stepped back, allowing Tom to drive forward. "I wonder if you should have given that phony name and address," Tom considered, turning toward Gwen. She might have gotten herself into trouble and there was still time to turn back and correct it. "What if they check and come after you?"

"They'd have to find me first," Gwen replied.

"Sage Valley isn't that big. You wouldn't be impossible to find. And they know you were with me."

"They won't bother," Gwen insisted.

Tom glanced at her from the corner of his eye as he drove out the school's front entrance. Despite her words, she looked worried. Gwen wasn't as tough as she tried to pretend; he'd gradually realized that in the course of talking to her at school. He wondered why she felt the need to throw up such a harsh front and remembered the rumors about her mother being gone. That had to be rough on her.

They were on Creek Road near the trailer park and about to turn up toward her house when Tom noticed an odd glow in the night sky. The moment he rolled down his window, acrid, smoky air wafted into the truck. "Something's on fire," he said, alarmed. "Maybe we should turn back."

"Don't turn back," Gwen said. "I want to see what's burning."

"I don't think it's safe," Tom objected, backing into Birchwood Lane and then turning in the opposite direction on Creek Road. They had to be crazy to drive straight into a fire emergency. "Let's go to my house and see what we can tell from there."

"All right," Gwen agreed, sounding reluctant.

They were nearing his driveway when they heard the first fire sirens. "It sounds big," Tom remarked. He knew that various Sage Valley volunteer firefighters responded or didn't, depending on how many siren blasts they heard. It sounded like all of them would be running for their blue-light-equipped cars tonight.

His mother was standing on the sidewalk, in her pink winter jacket and clutching a box. Quickly pulling to the curb, he leapt from the truck and ran to her. "What's happening, Mom? Are you okay?"

"I'm fine, but the house behind ours is up in flames," his mother said, her voice cracking with fear. "I grabbed this box of family photos and ran outside. Just pray it doesn't spread."

Gwen came out of the truck and joined him. "That's my house," she murmured.

"No," he said. But maybe it was. "Are you sure?"

Without waiting for her reply, Tom stepped into his driveway to check. Sparks, like fireworks, blew up over the high hedge at the back of his yard. By the time he was halfway up the driveway, he could feel the wall of heat.

The fire sirens suddenly grew loud on his street. Turning, he realized they were pulling in front of his house.

A firefighter in a yellow slicker appeared at the end of the driveway. "Do you own that truck?" he demanded of Tom.

"Yes."

"You have to move it. More trucks are coming. We're going to soak all this property back here and hope it doesn't catch."

"How's that house back there doing?" Tom asked, heading back down the driveway toward the firefighter. "Can you save it?"

"Do you think we can save that?" the firefighter asked scornfully as he gestured toward the flames dancing above the high hedges at the back of Tom's yard — flames turning the night's blackness into a purple haze shot through with orange sparks. "That old thing was a fire trap to begin with, but it would be bad if this nice block went up in flames."

Going toward the truck, Tom saw Gwen standing at the end of the driveway, gazing at the dancing lights of her home being destroyed.

What was that wild expression in her eyes?

It wasn't grief or fear. It struck him as something close to exaltation, as though she was actually happy to see the house go up in blazes.

"The house is gone, isn't it?" Gwen asked when he reached her, in a voice he found strangely bland.

"It sounds that way, yeah," Tom confirmed. "I'm real sorry. I hope Luke's all right."

"I called him," she murmured dreamily, not taking her eyes from the fire. "He's okay."

Tom scrutinized her mesmerized expression. For a moment, he wondered if she was hypnotized by the flames, or even in a state of shock. "Gwen, you know my name, don't you?" he tested.

She turned toward him, brows furrowed skeptically. "Of course I know it. What kind of question is that?"

"What is it?" he pressed.

"You're Napoléon Bonaparte."

He stared at her, not sure what to do next. She *was* in shock.

"Or maybe you're that dorky Mr. Ralph, who tried to teach creative journalism," Gwen added. Then the side of her right lip pulled up into a cynical grin. "I know you're Tom. What did you think? That the fire shocked me out of my head?"

"Maybe," he admitted, his voice taking on a sulky tone that embarrassed him. He suddenly felt like an idiot. "It's pretty shocking to have your house burn down."

"I was just waiting for this to happen. I've been telling Luke not to store gasoline."

"Like I said, I'm real sorry," he told her, meaning it. "Want me to drive you to Luke?"

Gwen shook her head. "I'm okay. I won't miss that house. It's not as though it was filled with happy memories."

In the next moment, Gwen's blankness fell away and was replaced by an expression of panicked worry. He could tell something new had just occurred to her. "I shouldn't be standing around here. This is a total disaster," she said, looking up at Tom, her eyes wide. "It's worse than you can imagine. There are going to be questions—about my mother, about Luke, about me. I'm not sticking around for that."

"What do you mean?"

"I mean, it's time for me to disappear."

All at once, the neighborhood came alive with the sounds of TVs and radios. Every house was illuminated. The streetlamps flickered back on in the street around them.

"The grid's back up!" Tom exulted. Closing his eyes, he soaked up the sounds and buzz of returning electricity.

He let himself enjoy this moment of relief before opening his eyes again. "What do you mean, 'disappear,'" he said, turning to find Gwen. "You can't—"

Turning completely around, he couldn't find her.

"Gwen!" he shouted. Where could she have gone so quickly? "Gwen!"

CHAPTER 9

Niki sat in the passenger seat next to a brunette named Stephy Rosen, who was on her cheering squad. As they drove down the street to her house, Stephy ogled the large homes lit with cozy front lights and Niki worried that Stephy might run up on the curb if she didn't get her eyes back on the road. "Marietta is so beautiful," Stephy crooned. "And it's great to be in a town that isn't pitch-black at night."

"It's okay. Thanks for the ride," Niki said. "I know it's out of your way."

"You're welcome." The girl glanced uneasily at her fuel gauge. "I'm glad you don't live any farther, though. Hopefully I have just enough to get home."

The dashboard was a blur until Niki bent closer and brought it into a soft focus. She was fed up with not seeing. "Don't tell anyone you saw this," she said, digging into her bag for the case that held her glasses. Slipping them on, she saw that Stephy had less than an eighth of a tank remaining. She took two fifty-dollar bills from her wallet and tucked them into the console between their seats. "Take this for the gas. Please."

"A hundred dollars! That's too much," Stephy objected.

"Are you kidding? Not for gasoline. It will only buy you a gallon, maybe a gallon and a half. The station on Main Street in Marietta usually has some, though there's always a long line. You'd better stop there before you head back to Sage Valley. Give my address if they insist you have to be from Marietta to get gas."

"Thanks, Niki. I wouldn't take it, but it's getting late and I really don't want to run out when I'm this far from Sage Valley."

"No, I understand. Definitely, take it."

"Good thing no one stole *my* gas."

"No kidding. Can you believe those guys?"

"Really! Hey, I saw you were with Tom Harris tonight. Something new?"

"Kind of," Niki admitted. "He's pretty hot, don't you think?"

"Very hot, in a quiet kind of way," Stephy agreed. "At least he's not all stuck on himself like a lot of the other guys on the team." Stephy grinned wickedly. "Is Brock crazy jealous?"

"I don't know. Was he there with someone?" She tapped her eyeglasses. "I couldn't really see until now."

"You look adorable in those," Stephy commented.

"No, I don't. Was Brock there with someone?"

"Uh-huh."

Niki stared at her pointedly.

"Oh, it was . . . um . . . Emily Mear. It didn't seem like he really liked her, though. He probably just wanted to make *you* nuts."

Niki pictured the girl Brock had been with. She wasn't even a cheerleader! It wouldn't last. But she knew Brock hadn't wanted to make her jealous. After all, he'd been the one who'd broken off with her—for the second time. She'd been dumped for Emily Mear? It seemed inconceivable, but . . .

"You're probably right," she assured Stephy. "He just wanted to get me upset. But I don't care. I'm really into Tom now."

Was that true? It might be. She wasn't sure yet.

She missed Brock and he'd been sweet tonight, though Niki wished he hadn't been. Brock was starting to be in her head less and less, and she didn't want him back there anytime soon.

"That's great about Tom. I can tell he really likes you," Stephy said. As she pulled to the curb in front of Niki's house, Stephy's phone lit and buzzed. "Oh, I forgot to turn it off before. I hope the battery isn't too low," Stephy said, reaching for the phone. No one in Sage Valley left their phones on anymore. They powered up, got their messages, then turned them off again, never certain when they'd have a chance to recharge the batteries.

Stephy did a small bounce in her seat when she read the text message. "Sage Valley has lights tonight. Yay!"

"Great!" Niki cheered.

"Just think, tonight I can charge this phone at home instead of sneaking into the girls' room at school to plug it in there," Stephy added, smiling delightedly. "No more detention for unauthorized plug-ins."

Niki checked her own phone, which still had half its battery life: seven texts from Tom, wanting to know if she was okay. She felt guilty that she hadn't contacted him sooner. *He* was the one who'd been in a fight, after all. She'd been so preoccupied with finding a ride home, and then she'd begun chatting with Stephy. He'd just flown out of her mind. She would call him as soon as she got inside.

The idea of going in made Niki turn toward her house. It was dark, though she detected a glow from the living room window. Was the gas fireplace still going?

A tingle of anxiety ran up her back.

Something wasn't right.

"Bye, Stephy. Don't forget to get gas," Niki said, stepping out of the car.

Stephy was smiling happily. "I can't wait to see the town with lights again. Everything's going to go back to normal now. I just know it is!"

"I bet you're right. Good night." Niki watched Stephy pull away and then turned, once more, toward her house. Zipping her jacket against the increasing cold, she approached the front door.

"Mom?" she checked, entering cautiously. Niki peered into the amber light of the barely burning gas fire. "Oh my God!" she gasped. The living room furniture had been flung everywhere. Shards of a vase lay shattered at her feet. A throw pillow had been ripped and its stuffing was scattered. An end table and chair lay toppled.

"Mom!" Niki called, now gripped by panic. What had happened here? "Mom!"

Then the truth struck her. Her father had done this.

Why had she left her mother here alone with him? She'd just assumed he'd calm down, but he hadn't. Clearly.

Niki hurried down the dark center hallway, kicking aside broken frames and shattered glass from paintings thrown to the ground. At the end of the hall was the family room, sunk down three steps so that it overlooked the deck that faced the lake. A voice emanated from the room. Stopping to listen, Niki realized a male news reporter was speaking.

Niki found her mother sitting on a couch, listening to a news program on a battery-operated radio. "Mom, are you all right?" she asked, entering the room.

Her mother kept her eyes on the radio. A reporter relayed the news that a Category Four hurricane had hit landfall in the Gulf Coast island city of Galveston, Texas. Meteorologists had named the hurricane Oscar. The winds were blasting at 120 miles per hour.

Niki couldn't believe what she was hearing:

"The real scary thing about this situation is that many, many people here in Galveston were willing to evacuate but were simply unable to find the gasoline necessary to make the trip."

Niki's mother turned to her. "Those poor, poor people, completely stranded there." Her red, puffed eyes made it obvious that she'd been crying. Was it her sympathy for the people of Galveston, or something else?

"What happened? Why is it so dark in here, Mom?"

"Your father forgot to pay the electric bill," her mother replied, her eyes still on the radio.

"Forgot?" Niki questioned.

"I don't know if he forgot or just didn't think they'd really turn off the electric."

"We have no electricity?" Niki asked, shocked.

"Not until we pay the bill."

Sitting beside her mother on the couch, Niki struggled to make sense of this. "Why didn't he pay the bill?"

Her mother laughed wearily as she shook her head. "As I told you, he's been out of work for the last two weeks. I thought we were living on our stock investments, but between the war in South America and the gas shortage, the stock market has been simply devastated."

Niki knew her dad was a stock trader, though she wasn't all that sure what his job entailed. No matter, though; she knew that the word *devastated* and the term *destroyed stock market* weren't good.

"You're okay, aren't you?" Niki checked. "He wouldn't hurt you, would he?"

Her mother shook her head. "I'm all right. He's sleeping it off now. When the lights went off, he had a complete meltdown. He's in a panic about money. Nobody's hiring." She sighed deeply—Niki had never seen her look so defeated. "How was the bonfire?"

Niki told her about the fight. "Everything was so crazy that I lost track of Tom. It seems to me that everyone is just cold and tired and looking for a fight these days."

"I think you're right," her mother agreed.

Mentioning Tom reminded Niki that she should answer his texts and let him know she was all right. She stood to go to her room.

Her mother turned back to the radio. A newswoman was speaking urgently. "This just in, meteorologists are tracking a Category Four hurricane that is continuing to gain force in the Caribbean off the coast of Puerto Rico. They have dubbed the storm Hurricane Pearl. There is speculation that by the time Pearl makes landfall in Miami, it could be a Category Five hurricane, which means gale force winds of over one hundred and fifty miles per hour. And what meteorologists most fear is that if Pearl sweeps across the Florida panhandle and into the Gulf to join forces with Hurricane Oscar, it could form a superhurricane, the force of which has never been seen before."

Niki knew she should feel safe, since she was over a thousand miles away from the storms.

But she didn't feel safe at all.

High School Brawl Results in New Teen Curfew

Fighting erupted last night at Sage Valley High's usually peaceful yearly homecoming bonfire. For years, visiting alumni have joined with students to become reacquainted and to celebrate the approaching football game between the Sage Valley Tigers and the Marietta Mariners.

At this year's event, tempers flared over several incidents of gasoline siphoning. Angry words escalated to violence when a tire iron was used to smash the front windshield of Marietta's team captain, Frank Hobart, suspected of instigating the siphoning. The window smashing was the catalyst for an all-out brawl between students from the two schools. Several students required hospitalization from injuries sustained before county police arrived to stop the fighting. Numerous arrests were made.

Several Marietta parents, whose children and vehicles were injured, threatened legal action. These threats were met with calls for countersuits from Sage Valley parents.

In response, the mayor of Sage Valley, Eleanor Crane, has instituted an emergency curfew, requiring Sage Valley students under the age of eighteen to be in their homes after eight o'clock. "This is a sensible measure, especially considering the general blackout conditions that have occurred in Sage Valley. It's just safer for students to stay inside."

Fire on Creek Road Still
Under Investigation

Sage Valley's night sky was ablaze two nights ago when an old-style wood-frame house off Creek Road caught fire. The cause of the fire is believed to be the improper storage of gasoline on the sixty-year-old home's enclosed front porch. Charred and melted containers containing small amounts of gasoline were found when firefighters arrived. These containers did not meet guidelines approved for safe gasoline storage and have led authorities to believe that they were used to store illegally obtained gasoline.

The homeowner, Mrs. Leila Jones, 38, a former bartender at the Happy Corners Lounge, could not be found for questioning. It has been discovered that Mrs. Jones relocated over two years ago to the state of Florida. Her neighbors said they've suspected Mrs. Jones was no longer at her home, but said that her children let it be known that their mother had taken ill and was bedridden.

Also missing are Lucas Jones, 20, and Gwendolyn Jones, 17. It is not believed that either of them was home when the fire started. The house, which was about to go into foreclosure due to unpaid property taxes, was not insured, so arson is not suspected.

Police tried to locate Gwendolyn Jones, a senior at Sage Valley High School, yesterday, but she did not arrive at school and her whereabouts remain unknown. Lucas Jones, known to frequent a motorcycle shop known as Ghost Motorcycle, was not located there, nor was he at Vinnie's Tattoo, another of his known hangouts. Police are currently searching for these two. They may face fines for the improper storage of gasoline leading to a fire, and are also suspected of selling black market gasoline, most likely at elevated prices.

Townships Brace for Worst as OscPearl Makes Way Up Eastern Seaboard

The superhurricane known as OscPearl, a combination of hurricanes Oscar and Pearl, hit land in Texas last night, knocking out nearly all the oil refineries along the Gulf Coast. Hardest hit was the robotic refinery set out in the Gulf itself. In this robotically "manned" facility, robots labor around the clock to extract oil buried thousands of feet beneath the ocean floor. Unlike the manned refineries that produce only several hundred barrels of crude oil a day, the robotic platform drills deep enough to produce over 6,500 barrels of crude per day.

President Waters has sent U.S. troops, including National Guardsmen, to the region, and he's called upon the Navy to repair the robotic platform, calling OscPearl "a national emergency of the first magnitude. Rebuilding the robotic oil refinery is our number one priority." But experts say that replacing the lost equipment, especially during the current oil crisis, will not be easily achieved.

In our area, experts expect OscPearl to lose velocity as it moves north. They admit to being surprised that the hurricane has not yet done so, causing incredible damage to the city of Atlanta before washing away the outer bank beaches of North Carolina. The inability of residents to evacuate due to gas shortages has caused a devastating loss of life in these areas.

Local municipalities in our region are laying in food and water supplies at local schools and shelters, but admit that food is scarce and costly due to the increased price of fuel for the trucking industry and the fact that fresh produce imported from Central and South America has been cut off due to the war. Fresh water is also in short supply. People are being encouraged to collect as much rain water as possible when OscPearl does hit, which is expected to be some time in the next four days.

Sandbagging along the Hudson River has already begun in an effort to hold back floodwaters. Though towns along the river tend to be elevated, trains on the Hudson Line, which run along the east side of the river, could be severely disrupted due to flooding. The many thousands of commuters who travel daily into New York City — and their number has grown dramatically since the recent oil and gasoline crisis — could find themselves stranded should the banks of the Hudson River flood.

While meteorologists keep their attention riveted to the path of this unbelievable storm, local residents are being asked to do everything possible to prepare for the worst.

CHAPTER 10

Gwen sighed and stuffed her phone into the back pocket of her jeans. Nothing but static. Every time she tried to call Luke, that's all she got.

She tried phoning the information number just to check her phone. More static. She tried the school — the same thing.

It wasn't her phone. It was all charged and lit up. She'd charged it at Ghost Motorcycle when she'd gone looking — unsuccessfully — for Luke.

It had to be OscPearl, Gwen decided as she gazed into the expanse of maples, oaks, and pines she was about to enter. OscPearl was probably messing with radio signals up and down the coast.

The woods surrounding Sage Valley might not have been the best destination in a hurricane — a *super*hurricane — she realized, watching the trees rustle in the wind. But she was here now and there was no turning back. She'd come to find the old mine shaft opening she'd remembered exploring as a kid.

It was the only safe hideaway she could think of. Staying with Tom wasn't an option. She wasn't about to involve him in her messy life.

She'd tried Hector's trailer, hoping she could stay with him, but he told her that a woman from Children's Services had been by looking for her already, and was coming back. Someone had told her Gwen and

Hector were friends. "Mom swore to her there was no way she was taking in a runaway and promised to turn you over if you showed up," he warned.

He'd given her a bag of salami, Oreos, a loaf of bread, and a six-pack of Juicy Juice. "Mom will notice it's gone and have a fit, but I'll pretend she's crazy and just imagined we had that food," he said with a laugh. "She's never really sure whether she's crazy or not, so it always works."

This morning, after spending a cold night on the bleachers at school, she'd noticed ominous storm clouds beginning to roll in. Gwen had heard enough news reports to know what they meant—OscPearl had arrived. Living out in the open was now out of the question. That's when she'd recalled the old mine shaft openings set into boulders in the woods.

Without further warning, the skies opened, releasing a torrent of rain. Gwen squinted into the blinding downpour, pushing her way against a brutal wind that had suddenly kicked up. She raised one arm to shield her face from windswept branches, leaves, and even stones that were sailing past her. With her other hand, she clutched the grocery bag containing food. Afraid the contents might get ruined, she bundled it more tightly, covered the bag with her sweatshirt, and entered the woods.

There was one shaft, in particular, she was searching for now, as she entered the sloping, tree-packed hill. Where, exactly, was it? Gwen hadn't been up in the woods that rimmed the valley in a few years.

The canopy of red, orange, and yellow autumn leaves cascaded to the ground. The battering of rain against the ones that remained above created an almost deafening din as wind tossed the trees violently back and forth. Gwen realized that the leaves were providing some shelter from the rain but fewer and fewer remained every second.

A sharp crack split the air. Her eyes darting upward, it took Gwen a second to fully comprehend what she was seeing. A giant pine had split three-quarters of the way up and appeared to move in slow motion as the top portion banged hard against its own trunk before bouncing free and spinning out into the air.

The disconnected treetop twisted twice, and then changed course, hurtling toward her.

Gwen stood, stuck to her spot, frozen in terror as it headed for her.

She sprang away at the last second, just as the heavy mass of wood hit the ground where she'd been standing. It then bounced, spraying wood chips and pine into the air, and finally hit the forest floor a second and last time, shaking everything around it.

Lying on the muddy ground just a foot away, Gwen allowed a frightened shudder to travel through her body. Tears sprang from the colliding emotions of terror and relief, and she let them fall freely, mixing with the rain pelting her face.

Gwen pulled herself to a sitting position after a few more minutes and searched around for the rough, irregular opening in the rocks that would lead to the mine shaft. As kids, she and Luke had played in these woods with friends. He'd been the one who'd pulled off the plywood boards that nailed shut the old coal mine opening so they could use it as their secret clubhouse. Companies didn't mine coal anymore in Sage Valley, and no one, as far as Gwen knew, had ever nailed the mine opening shut again. She hoped no park ranger had come by since her last visit.

There it was! Just beyond an outcropping of rock Gwen spied a black hole. Not covered!

From the ever-intensifying growl and toss of the wind, Gwen knew she'd found the opening just in time. But where was her bag of food? She'd lost it when the tree had fallen. She had to go back to find it.

As she scanned the area with her eyes, a second crack, this one louder than the last, told her another tree was coming down. She raced into the mine shaft opening just as a branch came crashing past her.

Gwen slumped against the inside of the crooked doorway of the mine shaft, built into the side of a hill deep in the Sage Valley woods. Rain poured in a sheet. The wavering image filtering through the waterfall in front of her was nothing but a blur of brown, gold, and red, with a few spots of remaining green.

A terrible howl filled the black, open space behind her, bouncing off the walls and rattling the loose, decaying stone. Gwen flattened herself against the wall, terrified. "It's just the wind. Just the wind," she told herself in a hoarse, frightened whisper.

Pushing back her soaked hair, Gwen shivered. Her hand came up bloody when she wiped it across her face. The branch that fell before she could get inside had cut her cheek. It stung like crazy.

Lowering herself to the dirt floor, Gwen let out a low chortle of grim laughter that began in her belly and traveled upward. Could things be any worse? Her situation was so bad that it was almost funny.

Almost.

"This will end," Gwen told herself aloud. "Storms end. Gas shortages end. Wars end." But she couldn't see an end to any of it.

Maybe this was the start of something new, a world of misery without end.

Outside, ancient trees fell, one after the other, smashing to the ground and shaking it, crashing into one another and shattering with the force of bombs. Rain pelted the leaves in a rhythmic tattoo that made Gwen imagine knives being thrown from the heavens.

She hung her head, shivering, letting the cold water from her hair and body soak the dirt floor until a mud puddle surrounded her.

How had this happened to her? Why did no one love her enough to come out to find her?

Pressing her forehead against her knees, she once again let her tears fall freely. She cried for the loss of the selfish woman who had been the only mother she'd ever had. She cried for the father she'd never known. She cried because Tom would never be interested in her, and she couldn't even figure out why she wanted him to care. She cried for the terrible condition of her life right then and there. She sobbed until she exhausted herself, and then she fell into a sleep that was just as sad as the waking.

Gwen awakened and immediately registered a change in the quality of the light coming through the mine shaft door. It was exquisitely clear.

There was no rain or wind. Just this strange light.

Standing, Gwen wiped her eyes and stepped out.

The scene of awesome destruction, breathtaking in its ferocity, was lit in the crystalline, white glow. Everywhere, trees were down — sometimes propped against one another, other times lying in piles of threes and fours on the ground. Above, the leaves had been stripped from the broken and bent remaining trees. The foliage floated in clumps in the puddles and raced along in small rivulets that had formed everywhere.

It was the most beautiful thing Gwen had ever seen.

Gazing upward, she saw a bright blue sky, but dark clouds hovered at its edges. It told her where she was.

Gwen was standing in the eye of Superhurricane OscPearl.

CHAPTER 11

Tom dropped down from his first-floor window, landing hip deep in filthy, frigid water. It rose nearly to the top of his father's old fishing waders, which Tom had donned for the post-hurricane exploration. The big maple in front of his house lay sideways in the brown torrent running down the street. Its massive roots pointed toward an amazingly blue, crystal-clear sky.

From across the street, Carlos hung out his first-story window and swung his left arm in greeting. His right arm stayed stationary at his side, encased in the plastered gauze of a cast and supported by a sling. His bruised face instantly reminded Tom of the fight at the high school. He could hardly believe it had only been five days ago.

Water was sloshing inside the waders by the time Tom reached Carlos. "Who ever thought we'd have waterfront property?" Carlos joked.

Tom grinned. "Yeah, who'd have thought it?"

"Now we're just like those snobs over on the water at Lake Morrisey," Carlos added. "I bet those houses are floating around in the lake now."

Tom wondered how Niki was doing. Her house was high up, so she was probably all right. She'd texted him after the bonfire to say she'd gotten home. He'd called her to apologize for leaving her stranded. He hadn't expected to become involved in a fight when he left her to check out the situation. Niki had said she understood.

And then OscPearl had begun moving up the coast, disrupting radio signals for hundreds of miles. It was off the coast of Boston now. Everyone was hoping it would veer off toward the ocean there and spare the rest of New England from its rage. It was still considered a Category Six hurricane. Tom's phone still wasn't working.

"You'd better get out of this water," Carlos told Tom. "You don't know what's floating around in here. There could even be live electric current traveling through. There are lots of downed wires. So if the power comes back on, you could get fried."

"I'm grounded from electric," Tom said, bouncing lightly in his waders. "Rubber boots. Electricity will run down the boots into the ground."

"Nice idea, but I wouldn't count on it," Carlos said. "For one thing, those waders are filled with water. I wouldn't bet my life on them protecting you from getting zapped. Besides, there could be all sorts of nasty stuff, including sewage, in this water."

Tom turned pale. "Sewage?"

Carlos nodded.

Tom boosted himself up into Carlos's window and Carlos helped pull him the rest of the way in. "Nice boots, Tom," Carlos's fifteen-year-old sister, Maritza, teased from the couch where she was reading a fashion magazine. "They're spilling all over the floor."

Carlos's mother came in, looking frazzled and tired. "Carlos, find some towels. He's soaking the floor. Maritza, get a pot from the kitchen."

Tom stood on the towels Carlos brought and, as gently as he could, emptied his waders into the kitchen pot. "Sorry, Mrs. Hernandez," he apologized.

"Whatever. Forget it. How's your mother?"

"Not so great this morning. She's trying to bail out our basement, which is completely flooded."

Mrs. Hernandez raised a skeptical eyebrow. "And you're not helping her?"

"She sent me out to see if I could buy a dehumidifier."

"What's she going to run it on . . . love?" Carlos's mother asked.

"She figures the power will come back on once the lines are repaired. We had power before the storm."

"I hope she's right, but it's not going to happen anytime soon, I can tell you that. Besides, nothing's open anywhere today. Tell her to come on over here. I have a little pancake mix left and some butter and syrup. I can cook us up some breakfast on Carlos's camping stove."

Maritza sat up on the couch looking alarmed. "That's *all* the food you have in the house?"

"Don't give me that look," her mother cautioned. "Have you been in the supermarkets lately? There's *nothing* on the shelves. The truckers are rationing their trips because of the gas. I stood in line for two hours just to get what I have in the house now—and it cost three times the usual price."

"I'm just saying . . . what are we going to do?" Maritza replied. "We can't eat pancakes forever."

"My mom has some stuff still in the fridge," Tom volunteered. "I think she wants to eat what's there before it all goes bad. If you run short, come over to us."

"That's sweet of you, Tom," Mrs. Hernandez said.

Carlos's father came into the room holding a hand pump. "The dinghy is blown up if we need to get out of here," he announced.

"Joe, could you take Carlos and Tom back over to Tom's house? Karen needs help bailing out her basement."

"Sure. Get some buckets, guys," Joe Hernandez replied. "Let's go."

After collecting buckets from a closet, Tom followed Carlos and his father back to the kitchen. Gazing out the window, he saw a yellow blow-up boat, large enough for four, bobbing in the three feet or so of muddy water below. The small craft was tied to the doorknob of the back door. "Out the window, boys," Carlos's father instructed. "Stay low in the dinghy. You don't want to tip and land in that muddy water. Who knows what's in there?"

Carlos went out first and Tom followed him down. Mr. Hernandez handed down the buckets and some oars before climbing down also. "Thanks for doing this," Tom told Carlos and his father. "Mom is going to really appreciate the help."

"No problem, Tom. That's what neighbors do. They help each other when times get tough," Joe Hernandez said, untying and pushing off from the house.

Every bump and small wave rocked the rubber vessel as Carlos's father rowed it around the side of the house and down the driveway. When they were out on the street, Tom realized immediately that the rush of water had increased by a lot. Joe Hernandez was pulling hard on the oars just to keep the small boat from being caught up and carried away in the current.

All around them, their neighbors were standing at their open windows calling out for help.

"My grandmother's stuck in our flooded basement. Help me carry her. Please!"

"We're out of food!"

"I've run out of my heart pills. I could die without them."

A golden retriever that Tom didn't recognize was being carried past the boat by the rushing torrent. The dog tried with futile movements to paddle away, but he was no match for the racing floodwaters. On instinct, Tom reached out and clutched the big dog's long, reddish fur. The boat rocked precariously as he hoisted the animal into it.

"Whoa! Tom!" cried Joe Hernandez. "What are you doing?"

"He would have drowned," Tom explained.

The dog shook himself dry, spraying them all with the foul water. When Tom stopped ducking away from the shower, he looked at the animal more closely and saw that the retriever was no longer a puppy, but still young.

"We've got all these people to try to help. We can't take on a dog right now," Carlos's father insisted.

"Maybe the dog can help," Carlos suggested.

"A dog has to be fed," his father replied.

"I'll take care of him," Tom insisted. He examined the collar the dog wore. There was no tag, but the name Larry was stitched onto it. "Larry," he repeated. "That's a funny name for a dog." He patted the dog's soaked fur. "Welcome aboard, Larry."

Joe Hernandez put his back into the work of rowing, turning the boat away from Tom's house. "Maybe we'd better see about that woman's grandmother, first."

Climatologists Now Believe OscPearl Caused by Global Warming
More Superhurricanes Could Be Brewing

Now that OscPearl has blown out to sea, scientists at England's University College, London, are busy studying the devastating super-hurricane. The conclusions they are drawing all seem to point in one direction: heat. To be more specific, the college's Benfield Hazard Research Centre is attributing the never-before-seen ferocity of OscPearl to the rise in sea surface temperatures that has been happening steadily over the last forty years—put even more plainly: global warming.

The researchers speculate that ocean temperatures may be climbing even more rapidly than atmospheric temperatures. A senior analyst with the National Hurricane Center likened warm ocean waters to the fuel for a car, claiming that just as high-octane gas produces more power, warmer ocean waters produce more powerful hurricanes.

Senator Thomas Rambling (D-MA) stated in a press release today: "As our state struggles to recover from this horrific storm, it makes us view the current fuel crisis in a new light. If indeed global warming is the culprit in the formation of this ruinous storm, then we must look to carbon emissions as the underlying cause. It flows logically from that, that the current unavailability of gas that has so curbed our driving and general mobility could be a blessing in disguise. We have just seen, in a wildly dramatic way, what our lack of leadership and grassroots action is costing us. Rather than striving to regain the oil that feeds our current way of life — and continues to raise carbon levels to dangerous highs, polluting and warming our planet — we should be searching for cleaner alternatives. Perhaps it is already too late, but we must try."

President Jeffrey Waters responded to Senator Rambling with harsh words. "This sort of panicky rhetoric undermines the current military effort to open oil fields in Venezuela and elsewhere. Oil is still abundant and continues to be the best source of inexpensive fuel. Without it, our entire way of life will have to be revamped in a way most citizens will find unacceptable."

Mr. Rambling rebutted the president's words, saying: "The last thing the oil suppliers want is for the American public, the world's largest consumer of crude oil, to wean themselves from their addiction to oil. We import over thirteen billion barrels of oil a day. Each day! For that reason, it has always been in the best interest of oil-producing countries to keep prices at a somewhat reasonable level. But now things have changed. Many of these oil-producing countries have finally, really, run out of what we have always known was a non-renewable source of fuel. Those that have some remaining supply are near depletion, though they don't want anyone to know it. This war with Venezuela is a game of blindman's bluff, costing American lives. It's time to stop the madness."

Senator Rambling is calling for an antiwar rally in Washington by the end of the month.

CHAPTER 12

Niki stood on her back deck and looked down the hill into the flood-waters. The family's Bayliner motorboat, still tethered to the family dock, was now completely submerged. The floodwaters had risen to just below the five-foot-high platform. But she could still see the boat sitting there below the surface.

Her glasses fogged, obscuring her view of Lake Morrisey, and she took them off to wipe on her shirt. Contact lenses weren't coming back into her life anytime soon, and there was no sense fighting the glasses. She needed to see, after all.

It was tempting to jump into the flooded lake. The water was mud-dier than usual with the contents from the bottom still swirling, but it didn't look awful. And she felt disgusting, having been unable to shower for days since the power shortage took out the electric pump to the family well.

She was hungry, too. In just one day, everything in the refrigerator and freezer was a melting mess. The stove and microwave were electric, so nothing could be cooked. Her breakfast had been a can of cold tomato soup, which hadn't been too awful, but now she was ready for lunch and didn't relish the idea of cold chicken soup.

After his rampage, her father had taken to his bed and hadn't yet emerged. Niki wondered if he even realized there had been a hurricane.

Her mother was staying glued to the radio, only moving away from it to rummage for something to eat. Niki had sat with her for two hours that morning, and was now more up-to-date on current events than she'd ever been in her life.

The war in Venezuela had escalated. Every day, more and more American troops went down to fight for oil. Bolivia had sided with Venezuela, and the fighting had spread.

A Russian nuclear submarine had been spotted off the coast of Nova Scotia, Canada.

The last BJK-Mart Superstore, in Danbury, Connecticut, had been forced to shut its gates when rioting broke out as customers fought over the sparse goods left on the shelves. The BJK-Mart corporation explained that not only was the high fuel price of trucking to blame, but also the fact that plastic was a product derived from oil and the elevated price of plastic products due to the scarcity of oil had made many of their products too expensive to stock.

Niki was still staring out at the lake when she noticed someone crossing the water on a Jet Ski. The water vehicle seemed to be heading directly for her. Niki realized it was closer than she'd originally thought. A teen boy was driving. "Tom?" she wondered aloud. It might be him, though she wasn't yet sure.

Descending several steps until her bare feet hit the water, she leaned out for a better look. It *was* Tom, and she laughed with delight at the improbability of his driving out to see her on a Jet Ski. As she waved to him, swinging her arm broadly, she snatched off her glasses and stuck them in the front pocket of her jeans.

When Tom was in front of her, he idled the Jet Ski. "How are you?" he called.

Niki had to admit he had the best smile.

"Where'd you get *that*?" she asked, pointing to the Jet Ski.

He put his finger to his lips. "I borrowed it," he admitted in a confiding tone. "It was floating in someone's yard, but their house was empty. I'll put it back when I'm done. Lucky the tank still has gas."

"How did you even get over to Marietta?" Niki asked. "All the roads are flooded."

"I used my friend's dinghy. It's tied up back there at the empty house."

"You floated here on a dinghy?!" Niki cried, laughing in disbelief.

Tom returned her laughter, shrugging in a way she found charming. "It got me here. I wanted to see you, and plus, I have something else I have to do."

"Want to come up?" Niki offered.

"Not now, thanks. I have this other thing to do."

"What do you have to do?"

"Get on, I'll give you a ride," Tom suggested. "You'll see."

"Okay," she agreed.

Tom brought the Jet Ski alongside the stairs and Niki came down another three steps before swinging around to settle in behind him. "Hang on," he instructed, and she wrapped her arms around his waist. Turning the hand throttle, Tom sent them surging forward into the lake.

Closing her eyes, Niki let the spray of lake water stirred up by the Jet Ski hit her face. Its bracing iciness made her feel alive, almost happy. There had been so much misery that riding so fast now with Tom made her feel that she could race away from it all, as though they might be able to actually outrun all the troubles of the world.

Tom drove them out to the north side of the lake. Speeding around a jutting lakeshore bend, he set a path toward a wooded island out in the middle of the lake. When they were close, he pulled up to a rotted dock extending off the island, half sunk below the water.

Getting off the Jet Ski, Tom offered Niki a hand in climbing onto the dry part of the dock. Then he pulled the Jet Ski up into the bushes. "Where are we?" Niki asked.

"Did you think you were the only one whose family owns property on Lake Morrisey?" he asked in a teasing voice. "This is my family's vacation estate."

Niki stepped up to her ankles in frigid water, and her bare feet sank into a muddy ooze as she gazed around at the trees and bushes, all tangled in vines. They were a blur, so she pulled out her glasses, intending to leave them on for just long enough to take in her surroundings.

The entire island must have been no more than ten yards long and about eight yards across. At its center was a tumbledown wooden storage shed, its shingled roof nearly crashed in by the heavy branch that lay on top of it. Its one window was smashed. "No kidding? Does your family really own this island?" Niki asked.

Tom nodded. "It was my grandfather's. I used to camp out here with him when I was little."

Tom pushed at the shed's jammed doorway until it gave way. He pushed through old camping equipment and boat oars. "What are you looking for?" Niki asked, stepping inside the shed behind him.

"Here's one of the things," he said. Gripping the top of a scratched orange canoe, he pulled it off the two wooden sawhorses on which it had been sitting.

Niki helped him pull it sideways out the shed door, the two of them struggling to make it fit through the narrow opening. "*That's* what you came here for?" Niki asked.

"Partly." He walked around to the far side of the shed. "Okay, here's another part."

Niki joined him and saw the bottom side of a small boat. "Is it a rowboat?" she asked.

"No," Tom replied as he turned the boat over, knocking out spiderwebs with his hands. "It's the hull of my father's old sailboat. It's got two sails—I think it's called a sloop. He used to take me out, and I could sail it if I can find the other parts. Right now it's completely disassembled, though."

Niki went with him back into the shed and followed his lead in continuing to overturn beach chairs and deflated floats to dig below moldy blankets, towels, anchors, motors, and just about anything anyone would ever need at a lake.

"Here it is," Tom said, pulling out a long metal pipe with nylon ropes wrapped around it. "The mast."

"What are those ropes for?" Niki asked.

"They're called halyards," he explained, still digging among the piles. "The sails are attached with them." After a few minutes more of searching, he unearthed two dirty nylon sails. "Aw, they're disgusting," he remarked, unfurling them on the shed's wooden floor.

"Did you plan to sail it?" Niki asked.

"Not today. It has to be fixed up. I'm going to drag the canoe home with me. This sailboat is too heavy, though. I'll have to come back for it."

"You're going to bring the canoe home on the Jet Ski?" she questioned.

He smiled sheepishly. "That was my plan, yeah. Once I get back to my dinghy I can attach it and float the canoe behind me."

"What for?" she asked. "Why do you want to bring it home?"

"People are stranded all around by me. I figure that any kind of boat that doesn't need gas would be good to have, and I remembered these were here."

"That makes sense, I suppose."

"Hey, did I tell you I have a dog now?" He told Niki about the golden retriever he'd found swimming in the floodwaters. "He must belong to someone, but he had no tags. All I know is that his collar says Larry, and he responds to it when I call him that. I checked with the sheriff's office to see if anyone's looking for him, but so far there's no news."

"I'm not big on dogs," Niki admitted.

"Oh? Well, I like him."

"I bet he's nice," Niki said, wishing she hadn't spoken, suddenly worried that he'd like her less for not loving dogs. "Larry is an adorable name. It's funny on a dog."

"Yeah," Tom agreed, gazing around the island. Suddenly, he laughed. "Don't I take you to the nicest places?" he joked. "First to an all-out fight between two high schools and now to a snake-infested island."

"Snakes?" Niki asked in a small, worried voice.

"Yeah," he confirmed. "They live all over the island. But they're not poisonous. By the way, did I say you look good in your glasses? I never knew you wore them."

"How do you know I—?" Niki's hands flew to her face. She'd completely forgotten she'd put them on. Embarrassed, she whipped off the glasses.

Laughing, Tom took the glasses from her and gently placed them back on her face. "You look good in them, and you have to see, don't you?"

"Do you really think they're all right?" Niki asked, sure he was just being nice.

"I think you look very pretty in the glasses," Tom said, putting his arms around her. In the next second, they were kissing.

Niki had never kissed a boy while wearing her glasses before. She'd never have thought it was something she'd ever do.

"Everything's changing so fast," she said quietly when they broke from their kiss. "I feel like I'm turning into someone else."

"Like who else?" Tom asked.

"I'm not sure," she admitted. "Does it sound crazy?"

"Everything is crazy now," he said, and then kissed her again.

CHAPTER 13

Gwen threw all her weight against one of the two huge trees, the one on top of the other that had fallen in front of the mine shaft doorway. It wouldn't budge. She screamed in frustrated defeat. She'd been pushing at the trees for at least a half hour without any result.

After the eye of OscPearl had passed, the storm had resumed, beating against the mine shaft with an even more terrifying ferocity than before. Gwen had rushed back inside and had been there mere minutes before the first tree crashed down and hit the second tree. She had cringed into a ball on the ground, covering her head and ears.

The two trees made a door that blocked the rain, and at first Gwen had been thankful for the additional protection, no longer fearing that her small space might flood. But now the storm was over, and the trees were stopping her from leaving the mine shaft. Initially, she'd hoped she could wriggle out through the space on top, but she couldn't even get her shoulders through.

Gwen's stomach rumbled and a dull ache of hunger was forming at its pit. Panic seized her, increasing the pain in her belly. What if she survived the storm only to starve to death, trapped here in this old mining shaft? Even if she shouted for help, who knew how long it would be before anyone came by? If it was weeks—and it could be—she'd be dead.

The small space suddenly felt unbearably claustrophobic. She had to get out.

Calm down, she urged herself. *Breathe.* There had to be a way out.

Searching around, Gwen saw a patch of wood about five feet square from side to side in the dirty rock floor—a trapdoor. Walking over, she realized that it hadn't been placed perfectly on the opening. And then a dim memory came to her. Luke, Rat, and other friends used to go down into the mine, leaving her on top, usually with a boy named Tim and his sister, Tina. Luke always said they were too young to come down into the mine, and Gwen had been just as happy not to go. The dark, rocky descent made her think of a fearsome entry into an underworld. As much as she would put on a brave face, she always sighed a deep breath of relief when Luke reemerged.

Gwen had asked Luke once if he could breathe all right when he was down in the mine. "Yeah, there's air down there," he'd answered. "It's coming from somewhere."

If there was air, maybe there was another way out.

Gripping the trapdoor's handle, Gwen put all her strength into pushing the door from atop the opening. The space between her shoulder blades cramped with the effort, and her biceps twisted in pain. She clamped her teeth together, contorting her face into a determined grimace until the door was pushed forward.

Breathing hard, she stepped back to observe her work. The door wasn't completely off, but she'd pushed it far enough for her to squeeze into the opening. Bending, Gwen peered into the blackness and another memory came to her—the secret flashlight. Luke and his friends kept it stashed on a rock shelf behind the metal steps leading down into the mine.

Did she have the nerve to go down there? Glancing back anxiously at the tree-blocked doorway, Gwen shuddered at the idea. What was down there?

But what other choice was there?

Gwen sat at the edge of the trapdoor opening. Turning, she lowered herself onto the metal ladder, feeling with her sneakers for the rung. Descending four more steps until she faced only dark rock, she groped through the ladder until her hand came to the heavy lantern-style flashlight she'd remembered.

Could the batteries still be good?

Clicking on the switch, nothing happened. Then she remembered something else Luke had told her. He always stored batteries separately. "They stay good as long as you don't leave them inside the flashlight," he'd told her. Again groping blindly for the rock shelf, she came to a blister pack of C batteries.

Score.

Feeling her way down the long ladder, flashlight clutched under her left arm, batteries stuffed deep into the back pocket of her jeans, Gwen felt as though she were disappearing into a world of utter blackness. The shaft opening above took on a grayish glow, lit by the bit of sunlight that filtered into the shaft from the opening, but it was disappearing with every downward step she took.

At the bottom of the ladder, she sat cross-legged on the cold, damp rock, which instantly soaked the seat of her jeans, and fumbled in the darkness with the bottom of the flashlight. When it was off, she loaded it with the batteries, feeling the bottom of each one with probing fingers to ascertain if it was going in the correct direction. Batteries like this had become rarer and rarer — and more and more expensive — in the past couple of years, but she still remembered how to do this.

Holding her breath in anticipation, she clicked to the ON position. Gwen blinked to adjust her eyes to the light as she took in her cavernous surroundings. The black and brown speckled rock was veined with bluish-gray lines.

Stalactites hung from the rocky ceiling and dripped everywhere. There was a sound of rushing water coming from somewhere, but she couldn't tell where.

When Gwen breathed out, her breath formed a cloud of vapor.

Swinging her flashlight all around, Gwen saw that the mine continued on to her right and she headed that way. Along the way, she scanned the walls with her flashlight beam, searching for anything that might indicate that there was light or air coming in.

After a while, Gwen's feet ached and she felt sure she had walked at least five miles. This endless underground path seemed to lead nowhere in particular. And now she would have to go back the way she'd come — because there was no way she was going to sleep down here in this cold, wet, dark place.

Throwing her arms wide in frustration, she swung around in a circle. And suddenly, she froze midswing, because right in front of her was a door made of a highly polished stainless steel.

Assuming it was locked, Gwen tried the handle just to be certain. And it opened. Pulling the door toward her, she stared in at the improbable sight of a clean, ultramodern living room. "Hello?" Gwen called, stretching forward to see more of the room. "Anybody home?"

The only reply was the hum of the stainless-steel refrigerator. Drawn by intense curiosity and the promise of finding food and water, Gwen stepped inside.

The door shut effortlessly, making no sound as it swung on silent, spring-loaded hinges. The room had no windows but was bathed in a pleasant, soft, whitish light from bulbs embedded in the ceiling. Gwen hoped this meant the power in Sage Valley had been restored.

At the room's center was a long, black counter space surrounded by high stools. On the right were couches covered in a tweedy, tan material and a smallish TV with about a 32-inch screen. A Ping-Pong table sat to the right of the couches.

Directly behind the counter was an all stainless-steel kitchen, and Gwen went right for the freezer, scooping a handful of ice into her parched mouth and letting the wonderful cold and wet melt there. This wasn't an illusion — it was real. Pulling open the refrigerator, she was deeply disappointed to find it empty.

In the cabinet, she found a supply of green-tinted drinking glasses that looked as if they had been made from the bottom of bottles, their edges smoothed. She took one and turned on the filtered water tap. She couldn't remember anything ever looking as delicious to her as the stream of crystal-clear water that ran out. Gwen gulped down an entire glass of it, and then refilled a second. It had been nearly twenty-four hours since she'd had anything to eat or drink, and the water instantly revived her.

A winding staircase in the corner of the room appeared to lead to an upper floor. Putting down the glass, Gwen went to the bottom of the stairs. "Hello? Anyone up there?" After waiting several minutes for a reply, she began to ascend the stairs.

Gwen emerged into a room flooded in sunlight; turning, she was greeted with a vision of the windblown forest, its downed trees nearly stripped of their foliage. It took a moment more of disoriented confusion for her to realize she was staring out of a window that ran from floor to ceiling and took up the entire wall.

Apparently, the underground path she had been on had sloped upward gently, bringing her just below the surface, and the staircase had brought her the rest of the way.

It had worked — she'd found a way out. But what was this place?

There was no other window aside from the one that covered the entire wall. Was this building set into the side of the hill? Going to the window, she pressed her cheek up to it, peered to her right, and saw nothing but rock. It seemed she'd guessed correctly.

The room was nearly empty, nothing but one long table on the highly polished wooden floor. There were three shut doors against the back wall. Gwen pushed open the first and found a small, windowless room she assumed was a bedroom. It was also empty, though there was an unfilled bookcase built into the wall. The second room was identical to the first, but the shelves were lined with various books.

Quickly perusing their spines, Gwen saw that they had titles such as *Building for a Greener Tomorrow, Straw Bale Insulation, Conquering Lift and Drag in Wind Power,* and *The Green Potential of Magnets.*

One book looked older than the others, and Gwen took it down. It was titled *Hubbert's Peak: the Impending World Oil Shortage* by Kenneth S. Deffeyes. It was an updated edition from back in 2003.

Thumbing through, she saw it was filled with graphs and charts. On the back cover, Gwen read a blurb explaining the book's subject. A geophysicist named M. King Hubbert, who was working for Shell, had predicted that oil production in the United States would reach its highest level in the 1970s, and after that, the production of crude oil would begin to fall off and would never again rise. Just as he'd foretold with the help of his complex mathematical formulas, since 1971 the U.S. had been dependent on the Organization of the Petroleum Exporting Companies for their oil.

He'd predicted this in 1956.

Gwen laid the book back on the shelf. 1956? It seemed that this mess they were in the middle of now had been coming for a long time. How had everyone missed the warning?

A low, humming sound distracted Gwen from her thoughts. It seemed to be coming from the next room. It was a whirring motor of some kind. Leaving the second room, she went out to search for the source of the resonance.

Pasted to the back of the third door, Gwen found a sign.

WELCOME TO THE HEART OF THE
WHIPPERSNAPPER 3
GREEN MODEL HOME—
THE REVOLUTIONARY MAGNETIC GENERATOR

The only thing on the floor was a motor about the size of a microwave oven, but with all its parts exposed. Four heavy plates spun, two clockwise, the other two counterclockwise. They were set between two heavy blocks of some kind of metal. It seemed that the spinning plates were turning two fan belts. It was all moving very fast.

Gwen turned back to the sign to find out some more about the Whippersnapper 3.

WELCOME TO THE HEART OF THE WHIPPERSNAPPER 3 GREEN MODEL HOME—
THE REVOLUTIONARY MAGNETIC GENERATOR

You have reached control central. For a one-time start-up cost of about five thousand dollars, a homeowner need never pay a single dollar more for electricity in his or her home. This amazing new generator from a visionary Australian inventor will completely power the Whippersnapper 3 home, producing up to twenty-four kilowatts of power per day. With an initial kick start from battery power, the generator utilizes magnetic attraction and repulsion to produce five times more power than it consumes.

We hope you've enjoyed your tour of the Whippersnapper 3 Green Model Home. From its third-floor greenhouse to its fully straw bale–insulated basement, this home is a completely self-sustaining answer to many of the fuel emergencies bound to face the planet in coming years.

Be part of the solution, not part of the problem. Ask your representative how you can purchase a Whippersnapper 3 Green Home today.

CHAPTER 14

Tom stopped in the second-floor hallway of his house to listen to the hacking cough coming from his mother's bedroom. Guilt shot through him. He'd left her there alone in the basement. He'd figured she was all right and other people needed him more.

And then, the next day, he'd taken the canoe out with Carlos and Carlos's dad, trying to help more neighbors who were stranded. His mother had gone down, once more, to try to bail out the basement. And now this morning, she'd started with this horrible coughing.

Moving to her door, he knocked. "Mom, can I come in?"

"Sure," she answered, which set off another fit of coughs.

His mother was still in bed and looked pale. "Have you eaten anything yet?" Tom asked her.

She nodded, catching her breath. "Some cereal."

"You found milk?" he asked hopefully.

"I had it dry," his mother replied. "Listen, there's not much food left. Can you go into town and see what you can find? And, maybe by some miracle, you can still get that dehumidifier."

Tom nodded. "Okay, yeah. It's cold in here. Do you have any other blankets?" His mother pointed to the top shelf of her closet, and he pulled down a woolen blanket to tuck around her. "I'll take the canoe out and go into town."

"Is the water still that high?"

"It's down about a foot from yesterday, but it's still high enough that the canoe is the best way to go."

"Okay. Be careful. There's money over there on my dresser. Or take my debit card from my wallet."

"No one's taking cards. They all want cash," Tom told her.

"Why not?"

"I don't know. It's just what I heard."

"Then take the cash. And get me some cough syrup."

Downstairs, Tom pulled open the refrigerator door. What a disgusting mess! His stomach rumbled. He counted the money in his pocket. Two hundred dollars. That should be enough to stock them up for a while, but he'd have to remember to buy only nonperishable items.

"Larry!" he called, and the golden retriever scampered in from the living room.

Tom ruffled the fur that curled like a mane around Larry's neck. Now that Larry was dry, he turned out to be a gorgeous animal with a thick, red coat. Tom hoped no one was looking for this dog right now. The possibility of giving up Larry was something he didn't want to consider. In only days, Tom had grown completely attached to him. "Come on, buddy, let's go find you some dog food."

Stepping outside to the back deck, Tom saw that the brown floodwaters were just about a foot below. He turned and began to untie the canoe that he'd tethered to the picnic table anchored to the deck. The table had withstood the blast of the storm, so he figured there was little danger of it floating off now.

He untied the canoe from the table, dropping it over the railing to the water below. Grabbing the oars from the table, he whistled for Larry as he descended the deck steps and grabbed the canoe at the bow. The dog came running, and Tom leaned aside to let him leap into the canoe. "Whoa, there!" he cautioned, laughing, as the canoe rocked from side to side. "You don't want to land in the water again, even if you are a good swimmer."

There was a strong current that required him to hang on to the deck while he climbed in, to keep from being swept away. The racing water carried him out to the street without even using the paddles. But then he had to stroke hard against the flow to turn the boat toward town.

Neighbors instantly noticed him and opened their windows.

"Hey, Tom, can you take me to the doctor?"

"I have money for food. Can you buy some for me?"

"Tom, the mold is making my sister sick. She needs to get out of the house."

"I'll be back soon!" he called to them. "I have to do something right now. A Red Cross boat will probably be by soon." Sage Valley had been officially declared a disaster area, but there were places, especially places south of them, which had been even harder hit. Various groups offering aid had come in, but Sage Valley was apparently lower on the list of places in need of immediate relief than others.

As he spoke, his words seemed to him shameful and cold. But he'd have felt just as bad if he helped them and ignored his mother yet again. "I'll be back," he repeated to no one in particular. He set his gaze dead ahead to avoid meeting any of their eyes as he threw his back into the task of rowing the canoe to town.

CHAPTER 15

Niki balanced the tray as she went up the steps to bring her father his lunch of canned chicken soup. She wondered if he'd appreciate the fact that she'd warmed it outside on the gas grill, using the last bit of propane left in the tank. Would the soup taste any different—smokier, more satisfying—for having been cooked outdoors? He probably wouldn't even notice.

Her mother usually did this, but she'd gone to see Niki's grandmother, who needed her medications refilled—and whose pharmacy hadn't reopened since OscPearl swept through. When Niki's mother had discovered she was out of gas, she'd taken Niki's bicycle for the four-mile trip. "I used to think Grandma lived close by," she said as she walked the bike to the puddle-dotted sidewalk. "Suddenly it seems like she lives far away. Not being able to drive certainly changes your point of view about distance."

Niki had nodded, though she hadn't particularly wanted to think about it. She still didn't want to spend time dwelling on any of this—not the aftereffects of the hurricane, not the war, not the gasoline shortage, certainly not her depressed, out-of-work father. Niki didn't want to spend time worrying about global warming, or about the possibility of more superhurricanes tearing their way up the coast. She was sick of hearing about all of it.

Niki just wanted to be left alone to think about Tom. He was a good kisser, a great kisser — better than Brock, whom she was surprised to realize she didn't think about much at all anymore. Brock's kisses had been sort of slobbery, now that she recalled.

It was pleasant to think about Tom, thrilling to think of him coming across the lake on the Jet Ski, to remember how his arms felt around her.

These memories almost made everything else go away.

But not completely.

"Come in," her father called in a sleepy, groggy voice when she knocked at his bedroom door.

"I brought you some soup." She hadn't intended for her voice to sound as annoyed as it did, but the sight of him lazing in bed, tranquilized, unshaven, wearing pajamas he hadn't changed in three days, was infuriating.

"Thank you," he said, taking the tray from her. "Your mother told me that storm I heard was a big hurricane. Is that true?"

Niki rolled her eyes and fought the urge to knock the tray over on him. "It was a *super*hurricane," she informed him stiffly.

"Oh, really?" he said, slurping his soup. "This is a little cold, Niki."

She ignored his criticism of the soup. It was too obnoxious to even acknowledge. "Yeah, a real slammin' hurricane," Niki said, her voice rising angrily. "The lake was halfway to the back deck. We *still* have no electricity, and now we have no gas for the generator, either."

"Go to the corner gas station and get some," her father suggested.

"Oh, you missed that, too. Marietta's private gas tanker can't get through the floodwater. There's no gasoline. No food. Nothing! And there's no way to get out except to walk like a bunch of refugees with all our belongings stacked in wagons or on our heads—and to where? No place is better off than Marietta, and Marietta is in big trouble. So you can imagine what the other towns are like." Niki threw her hands into the air. "Basically . . . we're all going to die."

Her father gazed at her blankly for a moment and then tossed his blanket aside. "If things are so bad, I guess I should get out of bed."

"That would be a start," Niki snapped.

"Sorry to leave you to handle it all. I guess I've had a sort of meltdown since losing my job."

"I suppose it's understandable," Niki grumbled begrudgingly. With everything that had happened recently, the idea of crawling into bed and simply staying there had a certain appeal.

"But what could I do about it all?" her father wondered aloud as he dragged the blanket back on. "What would be the point?"

"The point is that Mom and I could use some help!" Niki shouted.

"You two seem to be handling things."

"Dad, you're not an invalid! Snap out of it!"

Her father pushed the tray with the half-finished soup onto the bed and rolled over, facing away from Niki. "It's just all too much to deal with," he muttered.

Niki could only stare at his back, dumbstruck with disappointment. Then she picked up the tray and walked out. He had always seemed so in control. Was it his job that had been holding him together all along? How pathetic!

What held her together? As she walked back to the kitchen with the tray, she discovered that this was a question she couldn't easily answer. Nothing leapt to mind.

She didn't have many close friends. Was it Tom or, at least, the pleasure of thinking about him? Before Tom, being Brock's girlfriend had given her a sense of where she fit in.

Was it cheerleading? It *did* give her a sense of purpose—to her school, to her team. It was part of who she was.

But was that all she was? A cheerleader? Brock Brokowski's girlfriend? Tom Harris's girlfriend?

If those things were taken away, would she be just like her father, adrift and useless? Niki suddenly realized her eyes were wet with tears, and she quickly brushed them away.

This question was one more thing she didn't particularly want to think about. Only, somehow, Niki couldn't manage to put it out of her head.

CHAPTER 16

"This is definitely weird, Larry," Tom said as he canoed into the center of the Sage Valley business district. "Where is everybody?" Were any stores even open? He'd heard they were.

His canoe made a rough, scratching sound as it scraped the bottom of the road. The business district was at a higher elevation, closer to the valley's rim, than where Tom lived, so it was less flooded. "We'd better stow this thing," he told Larry as he got out of the canoe. Seeming to understand, Larry jumped out, splashing into the water, which came to the tops of his legs. He stayed by Tom's side as Tom dragged the canoe into some bushes, pushing the canoe deep into them until only a bit of orange peeked through. It wasn't a perfect hiding place, but it would have to do.

Tom slogged through the water with Larry leaping along at his side. The first store he came to was Maria's Deli. CLOSED — OUT OF EVERY-THING. HOPE TO REOPEN NEXT WEEK read the sign on the front door. The pizzeria he came to next wasn't open, either: PIZZA OVENS OUT OF ORDER DUE TO FLOOD.

By the time they were at the center of town, the water was below his knees. There were lights on in the post office, so he headed in. A line of people wrapped itself all the way to the door.

"No dogs!" the clerk behind the counter snapped.

"Aw, come on, man," Tom complained.

A hand shot out to wave to Tom. It was Mr. Curtin. "Give the kid a break, Les," he said to the clerk.

"Aw, what the heck. Okay," Les grumbled.

"Hey, Mr. Curtin," Tom said, joining him at the back of the line. "How's it going with you?"

"Hopefully better once I pick up this care package my sister sent. Everybody here is picking up packages. I guess we're the lucky ones. I can't even imagine how much it costs to send a package nowadays. How are things at your house?"

"Not so good. The water is still much deeper than here, and my mom's not feeling so good, either. She spent too much time in the basement trying to bail floodwater, and now she's coughing."

"I hope the mold in your house isn't getting to her," Mr. Curtin said. "I know mold grows fast in wet conditions and some people can get really serious respiratory conditions. I don't want to worry you, but you should be aware of it."

"I hope she doesn't have that. I thought it was just a head cold from standing in the water for so long," Tom said. Mr. Curtin *had* worried him.

"Maybe that's all it is," Mr. Curtin agreed unconvincingly. He took a pad and pen from the pocket of his corduroy sports jacket. "You know where I live. This is my cell phone number if we ever get electric and cell phone service again. If not, just come over if you need help of any kind."

"Thanks," Tom said, taking the paper from him. "When do you think school will open again?"

"Soon, I hope," Mr. Curtin replied, moving forward in line. "I'm desperately in need of a paycheck."

"I'm desperately in need of food," Tom said. "Do you know where I can buy some?"

"Do you know where the little A&P just about a mile up the road is? I heard that's open, although there's probably not much left."

"Great. Thanks," Tom said, backing toward the door. "I'll go there now."

"Okay. Good to see ya. Remember, you're welcome at my house anytime."

"Thanks." Tom motioned for Larry to follow him, and the two of them left the post office, going in the direction of the old A&P, built before the day of the superstores.

As they took the road back down into the valley, the water once again began to rise around them, and Tom wondered if he should have gone back for the canoe. He was a quarter mile down the road, looking at the houses, taking in the various kinds of damage they'd sustained. He came to one where a very large tree had come down right on top of a red hybrid parked in the driveway, crushing the roof on the driver's side. Tom recognized the vehicle.

Brock Brokowski came around the tree and waved to Tom. "How's it going?" he asked.

Tom shrugged. "Sorry about your car."

Brock shook his head miserably as he surveyed the damage. "I saved for this since freshman year," he lamented.

"Got insurance?" Tom asked.

"Yeah, but we've got no cell signals and even the landlines are down."

"I know. Sucks," Tom sympathized.

"Listen," Brock said, and an uneasy expression came over his face. "Have you seen Niki since the storm?"

Tom immediately saw himself kissing Niki there on the island and hoped Brock couldn't tell what he was thinking. He had no reason to feel guilty. Brock and Niki had broken up, and Tom had heard rumors that it was Brock who had broken it off. And apparently, Brock knew he was involved with Niki, or he wouldn't have asked if Tom had seen her. Just the same, Tom felt incredibly awkward. "Yeah, I saw her a few days ago. She's okay, I guess," he answered. "She's still living at Lake Morrisey."

"Do they have electric over there yet?"

Tom shook his head. "No, and that gas station that was getting fuel is shut down now, too."

"Man," Brock said with a sigh, "if those rich people over there can't get any help, what chance do we have? But you said Niki's okay, right?"

"Yeah, she seems to be," Tom told him. It sounded to Tom like Brock was still stuck on Niki. But if he was, why had he broken it off with her? Tom didn't know Brock well enough to ask. "I have to get going," Tom said instead. "Good luck with the car."

"Thanks," Brock said with a wave, returning his attention to assessing the damage.

By the time Tom and Larry neared the grocery store, the water was just below Tom's knees. The large, white building was in sight at the far end of a midsized parking lot, which was spotted with large puddles but was otherwise pretty dry. Tom noticed a vacuum machine about the size of a small car in the far corner of the lot, its orange hoses dangling, and assumed it had been used to suck up much of the water from the lot. This struck Tom as a hopeful gesture, considering that although there seemed to be about twenty people in front of the store, there were only three cars in the parking lot. He knew that right now most people couldn't get their water-logged engines running, and those who could start their cars couldn't find gas to fuel them.

He started to cross the lot but stopped walking when he realized that people were milling outside the store. Something about the scene wasn't right, but he couldn't quite figure out what. Then, suddenly, a man was knocked to the ground and Tom knew what was really happening. They were fighting. A curse was hurtled through the air as if to seal his new understanding of the situation.

A young woman ran toward him, pulling her little daughter along by the hand. In her other arm, she clutched a paper bag that looked half full.

"What's going on?" Tom asked the woman as she passed him.

"They're fighting over the food. The store is nearly out and closing down. Those who haven't been able to get any are attacking people as they come out with their bags," she reported.

"But you escaped? You're okay?" he checked with the woman.

"Yeah, I was able to grab this bag even though some spilled," she said without stopping.

Tom stared at her, aghast. She looked like a nice, normal person, a mother with her small child. *She* had robbed someone of their groceries?

"Don't look at me like that!" the woman shouted over her shoulder at Tom. "The kid is hungry. What am I supposed to do?"

Larry barked at her as if giving a reprimand, though Tom knew it was probably only a reaction to her agitated tone. He was caught between his impulse to avoid the fighting at the grocery store and intense curiosity. His curious nature won out, and he walked toward the front of the store.

Angry, shouting voices snapped in the air as he came close to the front entrance. One man punched another and sent him tottering backward so close to Tom that Tom had to leap out of the way. "You're not getting my food, you—"

Before the man could finish, the other man was off the ground and running back, his head bent as if he were a ram intending to butt horns with a rival, and shouting ferociously. The first man grabbed his groceries and began to run. He didn't get far before he was tackled to the ground by the guy he had punched, sending his food rolling out of the bag.

While the two men wrestled on the ground, three women and two men pounced on the spilled food, fighting to get as much of it as possible. Two of the women struggled over a jar of tomato sauce until it went flying out of their hands and smashed onto the parking lot's blacktop, spraying Tom and Larry. Larry licked his face clean with his long, pink tongue.

Tom saw that two boys about his age were shoving each other. He realized that one of them was the tall, Mohawked kid he'd seen Gwen with that day he'd been talking to Carlos by his truck. Hector. Maybe he knew where Gwen had disappeared to.

It didn't look like the best moment to speak to him. Hector was clutching his bag of groceries to his body while the other boy was trying to tear it away from him. "Hey!" Tom shouted at Hector's attacker. "Get your own food."

"Get lost," the other boy snarled.

"Why don't *you* get lost?" Tom countered, shoving the boy away from Hector.

As he staggered back, the kid glowered at Hector. "You're lucky your bodyguard showed up. Next time I'm gonna mess you up."

Hector just stood there panting as he hugged his brown bag of groceries. After the kid stormed off, Hector looked to Tom. "Thanks a lot," he said. "I'm not sure there's going to be a next time." He shook his head. "You know what I have in here? Anchovy paste. And canned corn. And pasta in the shape of unicorns. Basically, the only things left are the things that nobody ever really wanted."

A grocery clerk came to the door and quickly turned the inside dead bolt, locking the door. In the distance, a police siren sounded.

A heavy woman came flying between them, having just been pushed away from an abandoned grocery cart by another woman.

"Let's get out of here," Tom suggested to Hector after a quick check of the woman, who seemed to be unharmed as she ran back into the fray of people fighting over the cart's contents.

"Good idea," Hector agreed.

They walked to the back of the parking lot, skirting the wide puddles, without talking until they were far enough away to feel safe from the fighting. Two police cars came into the lot, their sirens screaming. Tom ducked his head away and noticed that Hector did the same. The last thing they needed was to be picked up for fighting in public; Tom supposed they would call it disorderly conduct. He had to wonder how the jails were functioning without power.

With a nod of his head, Tom signaled Hector to follow him even farther out of the lot until they were on a quiet side road. "Hi, I'm Tom," he said once it seemed safe to stop and talk. "This is Larry."

"Hey, Larry," Hector said with a small wave. "He's a great-looking dog," he told Tom.

"Thanks, I found him in the flood. Listen, we've never met and you don't know me, but—"

"I know who you are," Hector interrupted him. "You live behind Gwen. At least you used to before her house went up in smoke."

"How do you know where I live?" Tom asked.

Hector gazed at him as though filtering his reply, deciding what he wanted to say, and then he shrugged. "I think Gwen and I walked past your house one day and I figured it out."

"Of course, sure, I remember," Tom said. "That's why I wanted to ask if you know where Gwen is. I haven't seen her since the fire."

"I saw her after that," Hector revealed. "She was going off to find some old mine shaft to live in to keep safe from OscPearl."

"Are you kidding me?" Tom cried, alarmed. "And you let her go?"

"I couldn't really stop her," Hector defended himself. "She has her own mind. If she'd stayed with me, the cops or social services would have picked her up. Besides, right now, I'm living at the shelter in the basement of the elementary school. OscPearl demolished our trailer. I went up to the hills looking for her yesterday and the day before. I found a couple of mine shafts, but they were boarded up from the outside. There was no way she could have gotten into those."

"So where do you think she is?" Tom asked.

"No idea. Maybe she found Luke and they went off somewhere."

"She wouldn't have said good-bye to you? You're her boyfriend, right?"

"Did she tell you I was?"

"No, but I . . . you know . . . I assumed." Tom had meant to be casual when he'd asked if Hector was seeing Gwen. After all, it was none of his business, really. He'd just been kissing Niki yesterday. But he'd definitely detected a certain strain in his voice when he asked, and he wondered if Hector had caught it also. "Do you think we should go look for her again?" he suggested.

"Yeah," Hector said, "I think we should. I don't know where else to look except in the forest some more."

"I have a canoe. We can take it part of the way," Tom said. He whistled for Larry, who had gone off to explore some tall grass. "Let's go."

Tom tied the canoe to a tree, stowed his oars, and steadied the boat as Hector and Larry climbed out. They were all standing knee-deep in water but the canoe could no longer move forward. Without a word, they trudged up the muddy dirt road leading to the forest.

Tom's thoughts focused on Gwen. If she had been up here during OscPearl, how would she have survived? A mine shaft was probably good shelter, but did she have enough drinkable water and food? And OscPearl had ended four days ago—why hadn't she come down and let Hector know she was all right? "Why wouldn't she contact you? You *are* her boyfriend, aren't you?" Tom checked.

Again, Hector's shifting eyes made him seem to be calculating how he wanted to answer before actually speaking. Then a look of resignation came over his face. "If it were up to me, I would be," he finally replied.

Tom cast him a confused glance. "What do you mean?"

"I don't think Gwen is all that into me—I mean, in *that* way."

"But you like her?"

"Yeah."

"Oh," Tom said, absorbing this new information.

"Why?" Hector asked as they neared the trail leading into the hilly forest. "Are you interested?"

"In Gwen?"

"Who else are we talking about?"

Tom realized he was avoiding the question. *Was* he interested in Gwen? Niki was the one he was supposed to be involved with, wasn't she? And he *did* like Niki; he'd thought of no other girl but her for such a long, long time. But he'd found himself thinking a lot about Gwen ever since the night of the fire when she'd run off. Maybe he was just worried about her. But it felt like something more than that. "I don't know," Tom admitted to Hector. "I'm not sure."

Hector grunted noncommittally. "I'm not sure you're Gwen's type."

"Probably not," Tom conceded. *But still . . .*

CHAPTER 17

Gwen put down the fork she was using to eat the salad she'd picked from the greenhouse on the top floor of the Whippersnapper 3 Green Model Home and stared intently out the expansive wall of a window to the forest outside. Solid forms were moving among the trees. One? No. Two. Squinting for a better focus, Gwen could tell they weren't the white-tailed deer that often browsed by in their constant quest for leaves and brush to eat. There were two *people* out there.

They wouldn't be able to look in at her. Yesterday she went outside through the camouflaged sliding door and knew that the window panel was made of mildly reflective one-way glass. At first, all they'd see was more trees, and as long as they didn't catch sight of themselves in the greenish reflection, they might not realize there was anything there at all.

Getting up off the floor, she went close to the window for a better view. The forms were coming toward her. Were they hikers? Forest rangers?

No —

Hector!

Tom!

Running to the side door, she pounded the button that caused it to slide open and raced into the forest, calling to them. "I'm here! Over here!"

Larry barked and ran to her first, knocking her back a few steps as he leapt on her, infused with the excitement of her outburst. Gwen rubbed his head. "Hi, pleased to meet you," she said, laughing.

Hector and Tom ran to her. Hector threw his arms around Gwen, hugging her tight. "You're okay!" Then he gripped her arms, pushing her out of the hug for closer scrutiny. "You *are* okay, aren't you?"

Still laughing, Gwen leaned back into the hug. "Yes. Yes. I'm totally okay."

"Thank goodness," Tom said.

Gwen embraced him, too, her delight in seeing him making her forget any self-conscious inhibition. "Thank you for coming to find me. You, too, Hector. Thanks."

Gwen's eyes welled with happy tears. Someone had come out to look for her—two someones. She recalled the night in the mine shaft when the desolate feeling of being completely unloved and alone had been so awful that she'd cried herself to sleep.

Stepping back to look at them, she decided they didn't look all that great. Tom's bright eyes had a weary expression, and his clothes were dirty. Hector was even worse. His Mohawk had flopped to one side and there were dark circles under his eyes.

"How have you two been?" she asked, quickly brushing the wetness from her eyes.

"Not great," Hector admitted. "My trailer . . . like . . . just blew away."

Gwen gasped. "That's terrible."

"No kidding. It was terrifying."

"Were you there at the time?" Tom asked.

"Hell, yeah! We were there. The roof just peeled right off. The whole trailer park is demolished. We were able to get into my mother's car and just pray *it* didn't turn over."

"You were lucky it didn't," Tom said.

"It did turn on its side," Hector reported, "and it got blown down the road, but at least it didn't get far. That was the most horrible day of my life."

"What about you?" Gwen asked Tom.

"Our house held, but the basement is flooded and so are the streets. I guess it's because we're at the bottom of the valley."

"My house definitely wouldn't have lasted," Gwen realized. "It doesn't even matter that it burned. It would've been washed out or blown away."

"Maybe you should come to the shelter with me," Hector suggested.

"Yeah, and have social services put me in foster care? I don't think so. Besides, I have it good where I'm living. Better than you guys, it seems."

"Oh, yeah? Where *have* you been living?" Hector asked.

Gwen turned toward the reflective glass, but before she could explain, Tom jumped back, startled.

"Oh, man! What is that?" Hector cried as Larry barked at the reflection. "It's me!" Hector exclaimed as he walked forward to inspect his image. "For a second, I thought I was seeing a ghost."

Gwen stepped ahead of him and knocked on the glass.

"What's in there?" Tom asked, coming alongside her.

"It's the Whippersnapper Three," Gwen told them.

"The *what*?" Tom asked.

"I'll show you. Come on in. Follow me," Gwen told them, leading the way to the side door that was set into a huge boulder.

"You would never even know this place was here," Tom said, amazed, as he walked into the room on the main floor.

"I know," Gwen agreed. "Almost no impact on its environment; even the front isn't intrusive, as you saw."

Tom turned to look out at the forest, gaping in wonder. "Were we just out there? Is this one-way glass?"

"Yep," Gwen confirmed. "The Whippersnapper Three features passive solar design and natural cross-ventilation that eliminates the need for an air conditioner. It's made from all recycled and recyclable materials. It has storm water retention, and it all runs on a magnetic generator that never costs any more than its initial start-up cost."

"Awesome," Tom murmured.

"And that one-way glass," Gwen added, pointing toward the forest. "It's a solar panel."

"When did you become an expert on all this?" Hector asked as he slowly turned in a circle, taking in the Whippersnapper 3.

Gwen pointed to the pile of books she'd taken from the bookshelves and stacked on the floor. "I've been reading those, plus all the sales brochures on this place. There's not much else to do."

"So, do you have power here?" Tom asked.

Gwen nodded. "It seems like someone just left this house as it was and never came back. I don't think anyone ever lived here. It's just a sales model home. My best guess is that the people who built it live in California, or someplace else far enough away that it would cost way too much for them to move back right now."

"You have power!?" Hector cried, taking his cell phone from his jeans pocket. He cursed softly. "I didn't bring my charger."

"There's a charger rack downstairs," Gwen told him. "It's to encourage you not to leave chargers plugged in because they drain energy. Maybe you can find one that fits your phone. But come upstairs first. I want to show you guys something."

Gwen led them up a spiral staircase to the top floor. They stepped into a greenhouse brightly lit by natural sunlight pouring in. "I suppose you'd have to build a house like this in a clearing to get the sun in here like this," she said, "but isn't it cool?"

"How come we couldn't see this from the outside?" Tom asked, staring up.

"It's still below the outside walls, just the top is open. See?" Gwen explained. "The side walls use ultraviolet grow lights and those containers on the walls are hydroponics."

"Hydro what?" Hector asked.

"They're grown in the air without dirt," Gwen told him. "See the way the roots dangle down out of those holes? Every day a nutrient spray gives them food."

"How come these plants didn't die if the place was abandoned?" Tom asked.

Gwen pointed to sprinklers set into the glass. "Every day they get sprinkled with storm water collected in that cistern. There," she answered, pointing to a large blue bin on the outside corner of the glass roof. "There was a lot of rotten fruit and vegetables when I first got up here 'cause no one had collected it, which is why I don't think anyone's been here for at least a little while, but I just dumped the old fruit in the composting bin over there."

"This is awesome," Hector said, snapping off a twig of green basil and popping it into his mouth. "It's nice and warm in here, so I guess something is heating it."

Again, Gwen pointed up. "Those glass panels also work as solar heat, plus there are heating units in the walls that are powered by the same magnetic generator that's running the whole house. The panels must've been pretty thick to withstand the storm — but obviously they did." Gwen looked to Tom and Hector. "You guys look like you're hungry. Are you?"

"Real hungry," Hector replied.

"Dig in," Gwen offered. "There are some apple and peach trees at the far end in those pots. Hector is standing by the herbs. Tom, up in that container are hydroponic tomatoes and next to that, cucumbers."

"Where's the Twinkie plant?" Hector joked.

"Sorry, none of those," Gwen said, smiling. "Since I've been here I've been sort of forced to eat the good stuff. You get used to it, you know."

"Are these plants genetically modified to grow inside?" Tom asked.

Gwen shook her head. "No. They're totally natural. I've read a whole paper on what they've planted here. All these seeds come from a natural seed bank in Holland."

"A seed *bank*?" Hector questioned, snapping bright yellow cherry tomatoes from a plant.

Gwen nodded. "The stuff I read was real interesting. About thirty years ago, big biochemical companies started making genetically modified foods, things like square tomatoes that would fit more neatly into shipping containers. At first everybody was suspicious of it, but then we all just got used to it."

"I did a report on something like this last year in social studies," Hector added. "Didn't the companies make it so the fruits and vegetables completely died out each year?"

"That's right," Gwen said. "Farmers used to get their seeds from their crops. But now they had to buy them from the company every year."

"I read about that, too," Hector recalled excitedly. "They were called terminator seeds because they didn't renew themselves. Freaky."

"Yeah, way freaky," Gwen agreed. "So, then a few years ago, these reports started coming out by private medical groups claiming that a lot of the sickness they were seeing was tracing back to malnutrition. It turns out that the GMOs don't have the same nutritional value as the natural food had; only now there were no more seeds left. For a while, it looked like we had allowed the big biotech companies to destroy all the world's food. Except, fortunately, there were some groups that had thought this might be a problem and had begun collecting seeds."

"At least somebody was thinking," Tom remarked. "Is it hard to get the seeds?"

"Real hard," Gwen confirmed, "but the Whippersnapper Three comes with its own supply."

When they'd filled straw baskets with the food they'd picked, Gwen showed them to the basement kitchen. "You have to eat it plain because there's no salad dressing or anything like that here," she added apologetically.

"Are you kidding?" Hector said. "Do you know how good this tastes after eating nothing but powdered cheese and macaroni for days?"

"It's great," Tom agreed, popping a hydroponic strawberry into his mouth. "All I found was some stale cereal for breakfast. I had it dry and I haven't had anything since. It didn't seem like I was going to get anything else to eat, either, the way those people at the grocery store were acting."

Tom suddenly hit the table. "I can't believe I did it again!"

"What?" Gwen asked.

"I was supposed to bring my mother some groceries and medicine. She's sick. I was supposed to go right back, and I've been gone for at least three hours."

"I'll go get her some veggies and fruit," Gwen offered. "There's a bottle of acetaminophen in the medicine cabinet. You can bring that to her."

"Thanks."

"You know," Gwen began thoughtfully, "there's a lot of food up there that people could use. I wonder if you guys should tell them about this place."

"And have them duking it out in the forest?" Hector questioned. "You should have seen them, Gwen. They were clobbering each other for a bag of groceries. It was nuts."

"Way nuts," Tom agreed, shoveling a forkful of lettuce into his mouth while he hand-fed Larry snap peas, which the dog eagerly gobbled. "But I guess people get sort of crazy when they're hungry, especially people with kids."

"We have to find a way to get some of this food to them," Gwen said.

"Since when are you such a saint?" Hector asked lightly. "I thought you found people annoying."

"People *are* annoying," Gwen agreed. "But little kids shouldn't go hungry."

"True that," Hector agreed. "If you could fill a bag, I'll take it to the people in the shelter. I can say that I was abducted by a spaceship and the aliens returned me to earth with a bag of food as payment for the valuable internal body parts they stole from me."

"Okay," Gwen agreed.

"If you have extra, some of my neighbors are completely out of food," Tom added. "I'll say I got it in town somewhere."

"Why didn't I think of that?" Hector said.

"That's not the way your mind works," Gwen suggested.

"I have to ask you guys something," Hector continued, looking bothered by what he was about to say. "Is it just me, or does it feel like it's the end of the world?"

"Why should it be the end of the world?" Tom asked.

Gwen thought she understood what Hector was getting at. "It's as though the world is falling apart, and no one is in charge or even knows what to do about it."

"Exactly," Hector agreed.

"But is it the end of the world, or only the end of the world as we've always known it?" Tom considered.

Gwen looked at him as though suddenly seeing him in an entirely different way. Even though she had always liked him, she'd assumed he wasn't a person who would ever ask a question like that. He was a football player, not a deep thinker.

It struck her that she had made the same quick judgments about Tom that she so deeply resented others making about her.

"It's the end of the world," Hector decided.

"You could be right," Gwen said. "Or maybe it's just that everything about the way we live is going to have to change."

"What? Are we going to have to walk everywhere and become farmers?" Hector asked. "I don't know if I'm really into that."

"Me, neither," Gwen agreed. "But we might have to do that. Or at least ride bikes. I keep asking myself—is this a good thing or a bad thing that's happening?"

The three of them stared at one another helplessly.

"I have no idea about that," Tom admitted. "No idea at all."

"There's something else I want to show you in the back of this place," Gwen said. "It's a thing I've been building from some blueprints in a kit I found down here."

"A kit for what?" Tom asked.

"A still," Gwen replied.

"Like back in the days of prohibition when alcohol was illegal and they made whiskey in stills?" Hector asked quizzically.

"Sort of," Gwen answered.

"Gwen, don't tell me you've been out here getting blitzed every day," Hector said disapprovingly.

Gwen laughed. "No, crazy. Don't worry. I haven't been making whiskey. I've learned how to make alcohol for fuel—ethanol. Come on. I'll show you. It's pretty cool."

Mysterious Donations of Fresh Produce Bewilder Local Residents

Flood-stricken residents of Sage Valley have had at least a taste of good fortune to help ease the long, hard slog to recovery after Superhurricane OscPearl devastated much of their semirural town almost a week ago.

Desperately in need of services but largely overlooked by agencies busy assisting even harder hit areas, the citizens of Sage Valley are currently suffering from homelessness, flood-related respiratory diseases, and other sicknesses, plus an almost complete breakdown in their deliveries by rail and truck routes, resulting in a severely depleted supply of food and goods. Badly needed pharmaceuticals are also in short supply. Sage Valley is a town that can be excused for feeling that their government and even their neighboring towns have completely abandoned them.

But they have not been totally overlooked. Sage Valley residents have been pleasantly surprised to find gift baskets of fresh fruits and vegetables deposited at their front doors. Speculation is that the mysterious benefactor bestowing these much-needed foods must be a local resident with an insider's knowledge of Sage Valley's people, since the baskets have found their way to the elderly, sick, and families with children more quickly than to other townspeople who are more able to find food for themselves. Mayor Eleanor Crane tells us, "This must be someone with access to the food markets at Hunts Point in the Bronx. It's late September, and therefore these products have to be imported since it would be impossible to grow them locally at this time of year." Ms. Crane admits that her analysis does not take into consideration the fact that a person bringing food from Hunts Point would have to travel through areas that OscPearl has made impassable. "Perhaps this individual has a boat," Ms. Crane speculated. "Folks have told me about a person seen traveling around Sage Valley in an orange canoe."

CHAPTER 18

Niki heard the story about the "mysterious benefactor" in the orange canoe on her mother's radio, and thought, *Okay, so Tom is alive.* She knew there was no way to know whether he'd called her—her phone was dead—but still . . . he knew where she lived.

The last time she'd seen him, he'd seemed so crazy about her. Had all that meant nothing?

If he didn't come to see her soon, she might be gone. Most of her neighbors had left, though she wasn't exactly sure where they were leaving to. They said they were too isolated out here by the lake. Maybe they'd gone to relatives closer to town. Or even into the city.

Standing, Niki went down the steps to the wet dirt below. The lake had gone down a little, but everything was still so wet. Her glasses fogged and she wiped them on her shirt.

Why didn't all this water just evaporate?

The dark clouds overhead probably had something to do with it. The glorious days right after the hurricane had turned gloomy once more. The weather people said there were two more hurricanes brewing in the Caribbean. If they merged, it would be another OscPearl situation.

Everyone agreed: The East Coast couldn't take another superhurricane, not when it hadn't yet recovered from the first one.

Her father appeared on the deck in his pajamas, and barefoot; his face was covered in stubble and his hair bent at odd angles. "Do we have an oar for this kayak?" Niki called up to him.

"In that equipment chest over there," he replied, pointing to a rectangular cedar box behind the boat. "Where are you going?"

"We need fresh water and charcoal." They'd drunk the last of their bottled water supply. She'd taken some from the lake and boiled it, but then the charcoal supply slowly dwindled down to a few chunks.

"Wear a life vest. It's also in the chest."

Niki nodded and stopped to gaze at him a moment. Was he back from his stupor? He seemed to care if she was safe all of a sudden. That was probably a good sign.

"Okay. I will," she agreed as she leaned into the highly polished, wooden kayak, dipping her elbow in an effort to flip it hull-side up. It wasn't easy, but years of handsprings, cartwheels, and handstands had made her strong. In five minutes, she had dragged the kayak off its stand of twin sawhorses and pulled it to the shoreline, the back end afloat as the water lapped at its side, the front still in the dirt.

Niki ran back to the chest to get the long oar with its paddles on either end, and an orange life vest. "Take a chain and padlock with you. That's an expensive, handmade kayak," her father shouted.

"Okay." *That* was an excellent sign that he was getting back to his old self, Niki decided.

Returning to the kayak, Niki positioned herself low in the hull, stashed the life vest in front of her, and pushed off by digging the paddle into the ground. It was immediately exhilarating to be out on Lake

Morrisey, though the water was choppier than she'd expected and the breeze stronger than she had guessed.

Niki began rowing across the lake, knowing it would bring her to Shore Road. From there she could walk to town, even though it would be miles, and coming back she would be dragging charcoal and water.

Despite the difficulty, she didn't really mind going; she'd been stuck in the house with no electricity for longer than she could stand. If they hadn't had the battery-powered radio, she'd have gone totally insane. And even that was getting more and more static. She made a note to herself to also buy some batteries while she was in town.

This morning, the news report had said some towns not too far away had come back onto the electric grid and their power had been restored. Manhattan was the first to light up, though it was a mild amber version of its former illuminated glory, due to the necessity to conserve power. Towns in Westchester and the Bronx had power, too, especially the wealthier ones.

In lower Westchester, the floodwaters were receding enough for trucks to get through and bring in supplies. Train tracks weren't so flooded anymore, either.

But Marietta, Sage Valley, and other nearby towns weren't as lucky. What the reports had said seemed true to Niki: It was as if they had been forgotten.

When Niki reached knee-high water on the other side, she got out, pulled the kayak up, and stowed the oar inside. After chaining and locking it to a tree, she headed up a dirt trail.

Shore Road was eerily deserted — no cars at all. Listening hard, Niki couldn't detect even a single distant engine. The gray wash of sky above lent a somber, almost ghostly gloom. And there was a pervasive dampness in the air. Everything had gone silent and wet.

As Niki began walking toward town, her thoughts wandered and she remembered the day she'd been stuck there with Tom. Just a little more than a month and a half had passed, yet it seemed so long ago. It was as though it was a world away. Everything had been so different then.

When she even thought of herself, she felt she must have been a different person. In August, she was still the perfect girl she'd always been, the one with the swingy blunt haircut, the perfect skin — a girl who understood the world and knew exactly what she wanted from it.

Now, Niki laughed darkly at how that image contrasted with the girl currently heading down the road. This girl had unwashed hair pulled into a messy ponytail. Her skin now showed blemishes on her cheeks from a diet of canned and boxed foods and quick washups done by candlelight with water taken from the lake. She still had some clean clothing left, but it wasn't her first choice of what to wear. She'd just about gotten used to the sight of herself in eyeglasses when she'd dropped them one morning and the right side piece had snapped. Imagine, Niki Barton, captain of the cheer squad, in glasses taped together with a Band-Aid! It was almost funny — nearly hilarious, in fact.

Niki was nearly to the gas station that had been closed on the day she was out of gas with Tom when she spotted a lone male figure walking down the road coming toward her. Wiping mist from her glasses, she put them back on and peered at him. She knew those broad shoulders and his lumbering walk.

"Brock?" she asked.

What is he doing out here?

He started jogging toward her.

Niki knew what she was seeing was real, but it didn't seem possible. What were the chances of meeting Brock out here on the road like this? Her mind couldn't make sense of it. Back in August, it would have been a dream come true, but now Brock was someone who seemed like he belonged in that old world she'd left behind.

"Niki, why are you out here by yourself?" Brock asked breathlessly when he reached her.

"Me? Why are *you* here?"

Brock's crew cut was longer and he was thinner. He'd lost that square football-player shape that Niki had always found so appealing. But maybe she liked the look of this lankier Brock better. She couldn't be sure yet.

"I was coming to your house. I wanted to see if you were okay," he said, not meeting her eyes. His words surprised and shocked her — but they pleased her, too, and she wasn't sure why that should be.

"I'm all right. How are you?" she said.

"Okay, considering . . ."

"Considering what?"

"You know . . . all this. A tree fell on our roof during OscPearl. Another one came down and destroyed my car. My whole family is living in a shelter at Sage Valley Elementary. My little brother is real sick with some kind of pneumonia thing. They have all these cots set up in the gym for sick kids, but he's not going to get any better like that. The hospital says he's not sick enough for them to take him."

"How did you get all the way over here?" Niki asked.

"Biked. The roads are pretty passable now as long as it doesn't rain again." He shot a quick, worried glance at the sky. "Unfortunately, the bike blew a flat about a mile back."

"Sorry."

"Yeah. So, why are you out on the road like this?"

Before Niki could answer, a flatbed truck appeared on the road coming from down by the lake and heading toward town. Niki recognized it immediately. It was Tom's old brown truck.

"Where'd that guy ever get gas?" Brock wondered. "There's none anywhere."

Niki's heart raced as she tried to sort through the whirl of emotions she was feeling. She was glad to see Tom, really glad, but what would he think when he saw her there with Brock? Of all the moments for him to show up!

And yet she was so touched that Brock had come to see if she was all right.

The truck pulled to a stop right by Niki and Brock. Tom stuck his head out of the window. "You guys okay?" he asked.

"We're fine. Did you drive here?" Brock asked, going to the window. "The roads are passable now?"

"I came the back way, up on Ridge Road," Tom told them. "It's not too bad anymore."

"Where'd you get gas, man?"

Tom grinned. "I made it."

"What?" Niki would've thought Tom had totally lost it, if he weren't sitting in a running vehicle. "What are you talking about?"

"It's ethanol. I made it in a still from corn."

"Are you kidding?" Brock cried, impressed. "And this truck runs on it?"

"I had to tinker with the engine a little. I found this guy Artie, who showed me how to change the truck around. He used to charge a ton of money to do it, but he took pity on me and showed me how for nothing as long as I did the work."

"Did he show you how to make the ethanol, too?" Brock asked.

"No. Gwen Jones did."

"Gwen Jones?" Niki questioned, furrowing her brow with dislike. "That freaky Goth girl?"

"She's pretty cool when you get to know her," Tom replied.

"Since when do you hang out with Gwen Jones?" Niki demanded, irked by the way he'd defended the strange girl.

Brock looked at her sharply, and Niki knew he'd caught the jealous resentment in her tone. "I mean, I don't know her that well," she amended more mildly. "I just think she's strange, is all."

"I guess . . . in a way," Tom allowed. "But good strange."

"Whatever." Niki dismissed the subject, eager to be off it.

"Were you going into town?" Tom asked.

"I was," Niki said. "My family needs charcoal, water, and D batteries."

"Good luck finding any kind of batteries anywhere," Brock warned. "And how were you planning to drag all that stuff back?"

Niki flexed her bicep. "Muscle power," she replied.

"I'd have helped you, but it wouldn't have been easy," Brock remarked.

"Hop in," Tom invited them. "I can take you into town."

Niki climbed into the truck beside Tom, and then Brock wedged in, leaning against the passenger side door. *This is awkward*, Niki thought. But it was better than walking all the way into the center of Marietta.

An uneasy silence settled as Tom continued down the road. Niki was dying to ask Tom if he had come to see her, but it didn't seem right with Brock sitting right there.

"Is that your sailboat I see in the back?" Niki asked.

"Yeah, I came out here to get it."

A pang of disappointment ran through her. He'd come all this way and hadn't stopped by to see her. Though maybe he had. She'd have to wait to get him alone to find out.

Rain splashed the windshield and Tom turned on the wipers. They continued on without talking, the three of them staring into the gray road ahead.

Niki wondered if it was possible to like two boys at one time, because that was how she felt. If Brock wasn't there, she would have been happy to see Tom. But if Tom hadn't come along, she would have been thrilled that Brock had traveled so far to check on her. As it was, all she felt was extremely uncomfortable.

CHAPTER 19

"Why are Niki Barton and Brock Brokowski here?" Gwen asked Hector. She was staring in alarm out the rain-streaked wall-length front window. Tom, Niki, and Brock were pushing their way through the wet foliage, heading toward the Whippersnapper 3.

Hector looked up from the book on biofuels that he was reading cross-legged on the floor. "Who?"

"Niki Barton and Brock Brokowski," Gwen repeated.

Standing up, Hector joined Gwen at the window. "They're Tom's friends, I guess. That's what you get for crushing on a Neanderthal football player type—you inherit friends like Niki and Brock."

"Who says I'm crushing on Tom?" Gwen challenged. "And don't call him a Neanderthal—but that's not even the point. He's not my crush."

"Please." Hector brushed off her comment. "You've only been spying on the guy forever, and your face lights up every time you see him."

"That's not true," Gwen protested, although she knew Hector was right.

"Yeah, sure," Hector grumbled.

"Well, I don't want Niki and Brock here," Gwen complained. She especially didn't want Niki, Tom's dream girl, hanging around.

"So you *do* like Tom," Hector persisted. "And all footballers are Neanderthals. Who goes charging around smashing into other huge guys just to catch a ball?"

Gwen glanced up at Hector. "I thought you liked Tom," she said.

Hector met her gaze. "I thought *you* liked *me*."

Gwen put her hand on his arm. "I do like you, Hector."

"But not the same way you like Tom."

It occurred to her to sidestep the question by remarking that Tom wasn't interested in her, he liked Niki, but she knew that wasn't what Hector wanted to know. "Hector, you're my best friend, but I don't feel that way about you." She forced herself to tell him the truth, knowing how much her words hurt him and hating to cause him pain.

Hector nodded. "I had a feeling," he admitted quietly. "Even though I'm so much more your type."

Gwen wrapped him in a hug. "Sorry, Hector." She held on. "Do you hate me now?"

"Of course not," he mumbled.

"I'm glad."

"There are worse things than being friends, I guess," he said, squeezing her tightly. "Now you'd better let go, because I hear your boyfriend coming through the door with his pals. He might get the wrong idea. He already thought *I* was your boyfriend."

Gwen pulled away from Hector. "Did you tell him you were?"

"No! He came up with that on his own, and I told him I wasn't."

"You did? Thanks, Hector, you're a real—"

"Friend . . . I know."

Tom, Niki, and Brock stepped into the room. "This is it," Tom told them.

"Wow! It's like a secret hiding place," Brock said with enthusiasm. "You can't even see it from outside." He noticed Hector and Gwen and smiled. "I can't believe you found this. Unbelievably cool."

"Hi, Gwen," Niki greeted her. "This *is* very awesome."

Gwen realized how changed Niki looked and begrudgingly liked her, with her new, less-perfect image, a little better. At least she looked like a human being instead of a fashion doll now. "Cute glasses," she mumbled.

"Thanks," Niki replied, looking down self-consciously.

"Guess who we met on the way over here—Mr. Curtin!" Tom said. "And listen to this: His wife is an environmental engineer, and as soon as we have power again, she's going to start giving workshops to people in Sage Valley on alternative fuels and all sorts of stuff like solar and wind power. She's written up a grant to try to make the town a model of energy self-sufficiency. Is that cool, or what?"

Gwen put her anger aside as a new thought made it seem suddenly less important. "Why wait for the power to turn on?" she said. "We should have them come here."

It would be taking a big chance. If everyone knew about the place, it could bring all sorts of unwanted attention.

But it felt right.

"We can invite Mrs. Curtin to hold her workshops here, starting now," she said, her excitement growing.

Keeping the place to herself didn't seem to matter anymore. The private-world quality of the Whippersnapper 3 had been breached in her mind when Niki and Brock came in. No longer was the place her special, almost magical enclave to share with Tom and Hector. That loss made her a little sad, but there was no going back. The fact that it wasn't her secret spot anymore made her willing to open it up.

"That might call too much attention to the place, don't you think?" Hector worried. "What if the Whippersnapper people object? Or want their house back?"

"They're out of business," Gwen told him. "I searched them on the computer today. The company was owned by some billionaire's son who said he was just 'ahead of his time,' which is probably true. He's in Australia now, searching for something new to invest in. We'll take good care of the place until he comes looking for it."

"Once people find out there's food here, they'll all want to come," Tom said.

"There's food here?" Brock echoed enthusiastically.

"Go on upstairs," Gwen said. "Hector will show you."

"I will?" Hector questioned.

"Please."

With a nod to Niki and Brock, Hector led them upstairs to the garden. "You're angry that I brought them," Tom said when they were gone. "I should have thought about how you'd feel. They're not friends of yours and this is your place. I mean, you found it. They just seemed so . . . lost. I didn't think. Sorry."

Gwen wasn't sure how to respond. It was done now, and he hadn't meant any harm. One of the things she liked best about Tom was his openness and how he just jumped in to help people without calculating the risks. Gwen saw now how this quality might have its downside.

"I understand, I guess," she said. "They're your friends, and Niki's like, you know . . . whatever . . . you're going out with her and all . . . right?"

"Sort of . . . in a way," Tom replied.

"Did you get the sailboat?" Gwen asked, turning away so he wouldn't see how disappointed she was by his answer.

"It's in the truck," he told her.

Gwen sighed; she knew what he planned to do and it worried her. "Are you really sure you can sail it down the Hudson? Don't they have all sorts of heavy tides? I mean . . . it's the Hudson River. It's a big deal — and a small boat."

"I think I can do it, and I have to. My mom has pneumonia and no pharmacy in town can fill her antibiotic prescription. I have a bunch of neighbors who need their medicine, too. Down the river, things are better. There have got to be pharmacies open."

"Would it be better to take the canoe?"

"The sailboat is a lot faster than the canoe."

"You can't go by yourself," Gwen insisted. "I always wanted to learn to sail. I'm coming with you."

Tom gazed at her, surprised.

"Who will take care of things here?" he asked.

"Hector can do it. Maybe Brock and Niki will help him." Gwen watched his face carefully for his reaction to this idea. How would he feel about Brock and Niki being together while he was gone? However he felt, she couldn't tell because he didn't register any obvious emotion.

"I suppose so," Tom said thoughtfully. "But you don't know how to sail, do you?"

"Don't argue with me," Gwen insisted. "I'm a fast learner and you could show me what I need to know. I've felt kind of cooped up here, and getting onto the river would be awesome. So don't argue with —"

"I'm not arguing," Tom interrupted. "I think it would be great if you came along."

Gwen opened her mouth to speak, preparing to argue with Tom, but the realization of what he'd just said stopped her. "You do?" she checked.

"Yeah."

It was nearly a minute before Gwen realized she was standing there simply grinning.

"Okay, push it forward!" Tom shouted to Gwen, one hand gripping the boat's main line, the other shielding his eyes from the sun's glare.

"Are you nuts?" Gwen replied, speaking over the wind coming off the river. "I can't budge this, especially not with you standing in it."

They were at the public dock space down on the Hudson. It had taken them over an hour to unload the boat and rig it, setting in the one mainsail, tying in the lines, attaching the rudder, positioning the centerboard. Now it was on the ramp leading into the river, its bow bobbing in the choppy water but its stern still on the cement.

Tom rolled up his jeans. He'd already kicked off his sneakers. When he stepped out, the water made his feet instantly numb. The mainsail swung on its mast and bumped him, but he pushed it aside. "You get in and I'll push," he told Gwen.

"Isn't that sort of sexist?" Gwen objected.

"Somebody's got to hang on to the sail's line."

"Okay," Gwen agreed, running around the side and hopping into the boat. "Which rope do I grab?"

"It's called a line," Tom told her.

"So? What's the difference?" Gwen asked with a shrug.

"Hang on to the *rope* that runs along the mast," Tom shouted to her.

She looked at the center pole and the bottom pipe attached to it. "Which is the mast?" Gwen asked. Inwardly, she cringed at the look of frustration on his face. She grabbed the rope . . . line . . . whatever . . . nearest to the sail. "This?"

"Yes! That's it," he said. "Hold it loosely. Don't pull it tight or the sail could catch the wind and the boat take off without me."

"Okay," Gwen agreed, feeding more slack into the line.

"And keep your eyes on that sail. Make sure it doesn't whip around and clonk you in the head. That reminds me — get your life vest on."

"We're not even sailing yet." Gwen didn't think the life vest was probably her best look, and she didn't want to wear it in front of Tom, but the expression of exasperation on his face compelled her to shrug it on over her shoulders.

It occurred to Gwen that insisting on coming along with Tom might not have been the best idea she ever had. An inexperienced sailor on a rough trip like this could get him into a lot of trouble, especially when he was still trying to recall all his dad had taught him a long time ago about sailing.

There was no sense worrying about it now, though. She was here, and there was no turning back.

Tom threw his weight into pushing the boat forward. It budged slightly but not enough. "You're going to have to help me," he shouted.

"But the sail?" Gwen reminded him.

"Just be prepared to run," Tom warned.

The moment she let go of the sail's line, it began to flutter wildly. Gwen was lost in its folds, pounding them back just to get clear before ducking away. She ran back and joined Tom in shoving the back end of the sailboat. With the two of them pushing, the boat slid abruptly into the water. "Go! Go! Go!" Tom shouted.

They splashed into the icy river, soaking themselves. The sail flapped violently, snapping in the wind. Pitching their bodies into the hull, Tom was instantly at the rudder, pulling it hard with one hand while drawing in the main line with the other. "Lower the centerboard!" he yelled to Gwen.

"The what?" Gwen replied loudly just as the boat leaned heavily to the right, knocking her back. She gripped the side of the hull to keep from going overboard.

Tom nodded his head toward a board jutting up from the center of the boat's hull. "There, in the middle of the boat. That! Lower it!"

Lunging to it, Gwen found the lever that dropped the board down into the hull. The boat instantly righted.

"That stabilizes it," Tom explained as he continued to push the rudder to the right.

"Why aren't we going? What's wrong with this sail?" Gwen asked, pushing her windblown hair from her eyes.

"We're in irons."

"What's that?"

"The wind is hitting us from both sides, so we can't move forward. There's an oar on the bottom of the boat. Get up front left and paddle."

Gwen did as he said, and gradually she felt the sailboat turn. "Whoa!" she shouted as the sail suddenly caught, racing them forward.

They sped ahead, wildly out of control, for several yards before Tom was able to pull in the main line. "Stay low!" Tom said, gripping the white rope.

Gwen flattened her body against the bow and watched him pull in the line until the sail became tight. Slowly he gave it some slack until it was full with wind but under control. He looked to Gwen and smiled. "We did it."

Returning his smile, Gwen slid into the hull. "What should I do now?" she asked.

"Just watch me and I'll explain what I'm doing, and then later I'll let you try," Tom replied, getting into a more relaxed position, his right hand holding the main line and his left on the tiller that controlled the rudder. "Right now, we're running with the wind, which means it's behind us."

"What if it was blowing into us?" Gwen asked, settling into the hull.

"Then we'd have to tack back and forth, but I'll explain that later. Right now all I have to do is make small adjustments in direction to keep the sail full."

"How far do you think we'll have to go to find supplies?"

"We can stop at the first town where we see signs of electricity and check it out," Tom suggested. "I hope we don't have to go all the way to Manhattan."

"I don't think we will," Gwen said. "I heard Westchester is almost back."

Adjusting her position for a more comfortable one resting her back against the side, Gwen stretched her arms out and let the sun hit her cheeks and forehead. The sky above was clear with fat, white cloud mountains. Glancing outside the sailboat, she lost herself in watching the racing water splash against the boat's side.

This was what it once was like: boats pushed by wind. No hum of an engine. No fumes. The mercy of the river. The fate of the weather.

Was this how it was going to be again? Sailing. Walking. Planting. Growing.

The world was such a different place without oil. How would they survive without it? It seemed so impossible to go on.

Maybe it *was* the end of the world—*that* world, the planet where people lived by oil and died for it. At that very minute in Venezuela, some soldier from one side or the other was probably dying in this fight over oil. And no matter how hard they fought, it didn't stop the oil from running out.

Sooner, or maybe later, all the oil would run out—like it or not. Then what? No more gasoline engines, no more concrete, no more plastic. Not having plastic was as huge as not having gasoline, maybe even more so. What *wasn't* made of plastic these days?

Looking back at Tom, she saw he was also lost in thought as he lay against the back of the sailboat, his eyes on the sail but with a faraway look. He seemed peaceful, not at all like he was worried about this journey.

Gwen remembered seeing Tom in his yard the night his father died. Had that night seemed like the end of the world to him? It must have, in a way. It was his father who had taught him to sail. Was he thinking about his father now? Probably, she guessed.

On an impulse, Gwen shifted to the back of the sailboat beside Tom. Stretching forward, she kissed him on the lips.

Tom startled but then returned the kiss, pressing his lips into hers. "What was that for?" he asked when they pulled apart.

Gwen thought a moment, not sure how to put it into words. "Because I have a feeling we're going to the world that comes after the end of the world, and I'm happy we're going there together. Does that sound crazy?"

"A little, but I think I know what you mean. It's good that we're together, too. I'm glad you came with me."

"You are? Really?"

Tom nodded and kissed her again.

President Waters Calls Troops Home

Intelligence Reports Reveal Oil Fields in Venezuela Depleted

President Jeffrey Waters reported today that last week the White House received intelligence smuggled in by operatives from the nationalized oil fields of Venezuela. After a week spent verifying their veracity and analyzing the impact of the reports on U.S. policy, the White House has determined through sources that the reports are indeed accurate in their conclusion that Venezuela has grossly over-reported its oil-producing capacity.

Said President Waters: "Venezuela has cynically engaged us in warfare and dragged Bolivia into the fight rather than admit it has no oil left in its fields. Shame on them!"

In response, Thomas Rambling, senator from Massachusetts, had this to say, "Like Texas, Alaska, Canada, and the Middle Eastern nations before it, Venezuela has gone from oil boom to bust. This fact should be no surprise to anyone, since that has been the pattern of all oil-producing areas for more than a hundred years. The fact that Venezuela felt it could not reveal its new vulnerability as it drops out as one of the last oil-producing nations on earth demonstrates how the world is still clinging to outmoded notions about the status of oil-rich nations."

Senator Rambling, who has been championing the antiwar movement, had this to add: "When are we going to get it through our heads that oil is a nonrenewable resource? The future is in wind, solar, hydrogen, and other renewable sources like corn oil, magnetism, and the like. None of these alone can replace oil and so we must throw ourselves wholeheartedly into developing every source of renewable energy — nothing less than our survival as a global community depends on it."

CHAPTER 20

Tom pulled the tiller for a hard turn. "Coming about," he warned. Gwen ducked low, as he'd instructed her to do whenever he gave that command.

"Where are you going?" Gwen asked.

"I want to see what's happening. All these boats are going in there. Look." They'd come around a turn in the river and were suddenly amid many different sorts of small craft: kayaks; canoes; sailboats of every kind, from large sloops to catamarans, sailfish, and small fetches like the one they were on. There were rowboats and even people paddling smaller motorboats. "They all seem to be heading for that marina," he pointed out to Gwen. "Something must be going on."

"Where are we?" Gwen asked.

Tom checked the map he'd spread out at his feet. "This must be Hastings."

"Finally!" Gwen said, and he knew how she felt. They'd been sailing for almost three hours and every marina and port they'd come upon had been flooded or abandoned. The low-lying river towns had been hit the hardest by OscPearl. Many of the towns had overturned and sunken boats in their marinas, and harbor buildings with torn-off roofs and broken windows. It was frightening to see.

As Tom sailed in closer to the marina, he let out his main line and allowed his sail to flap, slowing the boat. It was necessary because so many other boats were crowding in around him. "What's going on here?" he asked a white-haired woman who paddled a blue kayak next to him.

"Farmer's market," the woman replied. "Some folks went down to Hunts Point Market early and brought up produce to sell. I heard it was all gone by five in the morning. But there are still soups, breads, ciders, and cheeses, too."

Tom's stomach growled enthusiastically at the mention of those last foods. He'd changed his diet in the last week. Never before had he eaten so many fruits and vegetables and actually enjoyed them, but a slice of bread and hunk of cheese suddenly struck him as too good to be true. "Is the town open?" he called to the woman as she glided forward away from him.

"Don't know," she called over her shoulder.

Dropping sail altogether, Tom and Gwen were able to tie the boat to the end of a dock that already held several other boats crowded and scraping against one another.

Tom disconnected the tiller and rudder as a safety precaution against anyone who might steal the boat. Throwing the tiller and rudder onto the dock, Tom swung himself up and extended his hand to help Gwen.

"This must be the only place with food for miles," Gwen said. "It's so crowded."

With Gwen beside him, Tom hurried up the narrow, sloping streets leading from the river until they came onto a more level street. When he found a small pharmacy, they went in and got to the end of a line that reached all the way to the other end of the store. The first thing Tom noticed was that the shelves were only half filled with the supplies drugstores usually carried, such as shampoos, soaps, and the like. Gwen left his side and grabbed a basket, loading it with necessities.

Tom fished his money from his front pocket and began counting out his bills. He had the two hundred from his savings. They desperately needed toothpaste, shampoo, toilet paper, and so many other things he had once taken for granted. He just hoped he had enough money for it all. They still needed to load up on food supplies.

Tom had other money besides the two hundred, but his neighbors had given it to him to pay for their medicines. In his back pocket, he had the stack of prescriptions to be filled.

"Thank heavens this place is open," said a man in his fifties who stood in front of them. "My wife could die if she suddenly stops taking her heart pills. I rowed all the way down from Monroe." He swung his right arm in a wide circle to work out the muscles. "I just pray they don't run out before we get to the counter."

"If they do, is any other town below here open?" Tom asked.

"I've heard that the towns south of here until Manhattan are pretty good because freighters are still coming into New York Harbor, but only about half as many are coming in because of the oil prices. Once you get south and east of the city, things get even worse. The Jersey Shore is just about washed away and so is Long Island."

"Where have all those people who were living there gone to?" Tom asked.

"Anywhere they can. The shelters in Manhattan are crammed full of them. Maybe now that this war is over, things will get a little better."

"Why is that?" Tom wanted to know as the line inched forward a little.

"The government has been shifting all the available oil to the troops. Maybe they'll release some of it now," the man explained.

"And then will people go back to driving all over the place?" Tom wondered.

"I guess," the man said. "People who can afford it will."

The man spoke about the return of inexpensive and abundant oil as if it were a good thing, but Tom wasn't so sure. What would happen the next time there was a shortage if nothing changed now? Maybe next time the oil would run out for good.

By the time Tom was nearly to the front of the line, Gwen was back at his side holding her basket of supplies. "You might have to put some of that back if I don't have enough money," he warned her.

"Okay," Gwen agreed as music began playing from the pocket of her sweatshirt. Pulling out her phone, her eyes lit excitedly. "It's Luke!" She clicked into the call. "Where have you been? Are you okay? I'm in Hastings. Hastings! Tom and I sailed down. No, I'm not kidding you. We sailed . . . okay . . . *he* sailed."

Gwen listened a while more and her smile slowly faded into an expression of distress. "Okay. All right, text me from now on—it will use less battery. Bye."

"What did he say?" Tom asked as Gwen put her phone back in her pocket. He could see from her face that it wasn't good news.

"A group from Marietta attacked Sage Valley."

Tom gazed at her, unsure he'd heard correctly. It was too crazy. One town attacking another?

"What kind of group?" he asked. "Who attacked Sage Valley? Why?"

A sheepish expression came over Gwen's face. "You caused it."

"What? Me? What? How could I cause it?" What was she talking about?

"Indirectly, it's you. People saw the news about you delivering food, so a bunch of them came over to find where the food was coming from. They wound up breaking some windows and they got into a big brawl with some people from Sage Valley."

"We'd better get back there," Tom said. He was thinking of his mother laid up in bed, and even of Larry. The Whippersnapper 3 could come under attack if people learned about it.

Tom had come to the front of the line and laid down his prescriptions. "I can't fill every one of these," the tall, dark-haired woman pharmacist told him. "Let me see what I can get you."

"Okay," he told the pharmacist. Then he turned to Gwen and said, "Let's get this stuff, grab some food, and get home. I have a really weird feeling something bad's going to happen."

CHAPTER 21

Niki sat beside Brock on the tan couch in the basement of the Whippersnapper 3. They were watching the informational DVD that Mary Curtin was showing to the twenty people who were attending one of her workshops. The video was called *Renewable Energy: A Do-It-Yourself Guide*.

Niki looked the group over. She knew about a quarter of them. There were several teachers from school, some were parents of her friends on the cheer squad, others she'd simply seen around town through the years. She also recognized Tom's friend, Carlos Hernandez. He was there with a man who looked like he must be his father.

A lot of the group members were fiddling with their phones while the video was explaining how to construct a small-scale wind power turbine to supply energy to an individual home. Niki hoped they hadn't just come to the workshop to charge their phones, as Mrs. Curtin allowed them to do before the workshop officially started. Sage Valley was still not back on the electric grid, and neither were most of the surrounding towns. It made Niki nervous that so many people now knew there was electricity to be had out here in the forest. They didn't need a crowd of people here all desperate to recharge.

"I want us to start small," Mrs. Curtin said to the group. "We're going to start by building small greenhouses from scrap glass and metal my husband and I have collected from the dump, or bought inexpensively from the car salvage and the recycle center."

Mr. Curtin, who had been standing in a corner listening, raised his palms, revealing red lines. "I have the sliced hands to show for it," he said.

"I told you to wear gloves," Mrs. Curtin reminded him with a good-natured shrug.

"That, you did," Mr. Curtin agreed.

"Let's have some of the fruit smoothies Hector made from the plants in our upstairs garden and then get started," Mrs. Curtin told the group.

The ringtone on Niki's phone sounded and she looked down to see who it was. It was a welcome sound, so good to feel connected to the world around her again. "Tom! Hi! How's it going?"

She felt a pang of jealousy as Tom revealed that Gwen was actually sailing the boat at the moment, but it passed quickly. Being here with Brock had been pleasant, and for long stretches of time distracted her from worrying about what was happening with Gwen and Tom.

Tom told her about the fighting in Sage Valley and advised her not to tell anyone else about the Whippersnapper 3. "Too late," Niki told him. "Hector contacted the Curtins about holding the workshops here. Mrs. Curtin was blown away by the place. And listen to this — she even went to grad school with Ricky Montbank, the guy who owns the Whippersnapper Corporation. But what are you saying about fighting? How can that be possible? Towns don't attack each other."

Tom told her what Luke had told Gwen. He was even able to send her a photo taken from the Internet of brawling going on in downtown Sage Valley, not far from the post office. "What do you think we should do?" she asked.

He said he didn't know and to ask the Curtins what they thought. "Okay. Where are you?"

There was a pause, and Niki could picture Tom gazing around the river embankments trying to ascertain his location. He told her it was foggy and he couldn't exactly tell, but that they were hugging the shoreline so they didn't veer to the far side of the river. There wasn't much wind, but luckily the little they had was blowing north in their direction. He was afraid, though, that the wind would die out altogether and they would be becalmed.

"Be-what?" Niki questioned.

It meant stuck, he told her.

"Maybe you should sail the boat."

He said Gwen was doing a great job; she'd learned really fast. He had sailed all the way down and needed a break. It was a good thing Gwen had come with him since she'd been such a big help.

Gwen learned to sail faster than anyone I've ever known. Tom's exact words rang in Niki's ears and caused a tingle of emotion below her eyes.

"Okay, Tom. Good luck. See you soon." Niki clicked off the call and blinked away the rising tears before they fell free. It was over between them before it really began; she knew it. It was in his voice and the way he said Gwen's name.

Getting off the couch, Niki found Mr. Curtin at the computer watching a YouTube video on installing solar panels. "Tom just called. People from Marietta are looking for the food they've heard we have here. It sounds like they're looting and just going crazy. People in town are fighting back and it's getting bad." Niki showed him the picture from the Internet.

Mr. Curtin picked his cell phone off the desk and punched in a number. "I'm calling the county sheriff's department," he told her. "Maybe I can find out what's happening."

"What's going on?" Mrs. Curtin asked, joining them.

Niki told her what she knew.

"I can't get through to the sheriff," Mr. Curtin reported. "I just get a busy tone."

From upstairs, glass shattered. Hector clambered down the stairs, his face full of alarm. "Someone hurled a rock through the front window!" he told them.

"It's those rich creeps from Marietta," cried a man from the workshop. "I just heard about it on the web feed from my phone. They're in Sage Valley to steal our supplies."

"We have to fight them," a woman said.

"Maybe we can talk to them calmly," Mr. Curtin suggested.

"You can't talk to a mob," another of the men disagreed as he found a large kitchen knife among the supplies.

Hector scrambled down the stairway and hurried toward the side door that led to the mining tunnel Gwen had shown him. "We can get out this way. It can be locked behind us. We can climb up into the mine shaft. The way out is blocked, but you can be safe there until these Marietta guys leave."

"I'm not running like a coward," a man from the workshop objected.

"I'm going," said a white-haired woman. "This isn't my house. I don't need to defend it."

Another sound of shattering glass made Niki jump.

"Those solar panels are going to cost a lot to replace," Mrs. Curtin worried. "We have to stop them."

Brock stood beside Mr. Curtin. "I'll go up there and try to talk to them," he volunteered.

Carlos stood and joined Brock. "I'll go with you," he said.

"No, it's too dangerous," Mrs. Curtin disagreed.

"I'll go with him, too," Niki said.

Brock looked at her, surprised.

"I have a house in Marietta. Maybe I'll know some of the people and I can talk to them," Niki said. "They'll see me as a neighbor, maybe."

"Are you crazy?" a man from the workshop said. "Those people are throwing rocks. You'll get killed."

"Well, I'm not standing down here waiting to be killed," said the man with the kitchen knife.

Mr. Curtin raised his arms to settle the crowd. "No one will get killed or even hurt if we keep our heads. Hector, open the door and let anyone out who wants to leave."

Hector pulled the door open and eleven people left quickly. "Remember to lock it shut from your side," he reminded the last one out.

"You're not going?" Brock asked Hector.

"No way," he replied. "And miss all this action? Never."

Mr. Curtin headed toward the stairs and started going up. Mary Curtin joined him, and the rest of the remaining nine from the Sage Valley workshop group followed.

More glass broke and now Niki could hear frantic, excited voices coming from upstairs. "They're almost in," Hector reported from the top of the stairs.

Frightened, Niki took Brock's hand. With his worried eyes still on the stairs, Brock squeezed it and kept walking with her.

On the first floor, Niki stepped back in fear, still clutching Brock's hand. Broken glass lay all over the floor and people were starting to climb through the shattered front panes.

"They have electricity in here!" shouted a balding man in a sweatshirt and jeans as he knocked the jagged shards of glass from the windowpanes with an ax. "Come on!"

Behind him were at least twenty people, some with rocks in their hands, ready to stampede in.

"Please, everyone, calm down!" Mr. Curtin implored as he went toward the broken window. "Stay calm and there's enough here for everyone."

"Then why haven't you shared it already?" shouted a woman outside. Mr. Curtin turned toward her voice just as a rock hit him in the head, knocking him into his wife. A line of blood gushed from his forehead.

"That's it!" cried the man with the kitchen knife. "We're not going to just stand here and take this!" The people behind surged forward but then stopped abruptly.

The sound of roaring engines came toward them. It took a moment for Niki to realize what was crashing through the woods toward them. The Marietta people outside were equally stunned by the sight, frozen where they stood.

A motorcycle pulled up in front of the Whippersnapper 3 and a leather-clad male figure jumped from his bike. When the rider pushed back the visor on his helmet, Niki recognized him. "That's Gwen's brother," she told Brock.

"Just in time," Brock remarked. "I'm going to help him."

"I'll come with you," Niki said.

"No — stay back here," Brock disagreed, letting go of her hand.

Niki let him get a few paces ahead and then followed him toward the window. Kicking away more sharp glass at the panes, Brock stepped out behind Luke, and Carlos went out behind him. Her heart pounding with fear, Niki went out, too.

Looking to both sides, she saw about ten other bikers. They held clubs and chains in a successful effort to appear as menacing as possible. "You people are invading private property," Luke said, "and me and my buddies are here to make sure you don't."

In the distance, the wail of police sirens could be heard.

Niki ducked her head as a tremendous wind shook the trees. A police helicopter hovered just above the trees.

"Oh, and did I mention the police are on their way?" Luke shouted over the thundering of the police chopper.

NORTH COUNTRY NEWS

County Police Clamp Down on Civil Violence Connected to Severe Shortages

Sage County police arrested eighty-one people recently in connection to outbreaks of civil unrest due to the fact that so many towns in Sage County have been without electricity and other services since OscPearl decimated the area over two weeks ago.

In one of the most shocking displays of violence, close to approximately fifty citizens of Marietta township descended on the semirural town of Sage Valley—many of them on foot due to the current ongoing gas shortage—in search of much-needed food, medicine, and other goods that have been unavailable in Marietta since the hurricane struck. George Amos of Marietta, speaking from the county jail, made this statement to the press: "We came because we read the article about the mysterious guy in the orange canoe delivering fresh produce. Our kids are hungry and sick. We figured if he had food to deliver, there must be more of it. We came intending to buy it, but when we couldn't find anything, I guess we got crazy."

CHAPTER 22

Saturday morning, Gwen rolled over and gazed around her small bedroom in the Whippersnapper 3. She'd been staying there with the Curtins ever since she and Tom returned from their journey downriver two weeks earlier. They'd sailed at least a dozen more times since then, each time having to go less and less far since towns closer to home were beginning to recover.

Next door, she could hear the hum of the magnetic generator and she found it comforting to know she would have heat and light on that chilly October morning. She knew it would be brisk out because they'd been checking the weather report frequently, hoping for a good day. Hopefully, it would be sunny and cool, just as reported.

Outside her room, she heard voices talking amiably. The robust and distinctly Australian tones of Ricky Montbank, owner of the Whippersnapper 3, could be heard above those of Mr. and Mrs. Curtin. "I'm glad to do it, Mary," he was saying to Mrs. Curtin. "I think what you want to do is remarkable, and my Whippersnapper Corporation is delighted to support it. This event today will bring lots of attention to the company."

"That's not really why we're doing it," Mrs. Curtin said. "You understand that, don't you, Ricky? We just believe it's the right thing to do."

"Of course! Of course it's the right thing."

"So no press," Mr. Curtin requested. "Please. We don't want anyone to be embarrassed. Folks in Marietta are used to being on the winning side, and we don't want them humiliated by this."

"Oh, all right," Ricky Montbank said, relenting. "But if you're going to make Sage Valley a showcase for green living, you have to be more publicity oriented. I'm letting you all stay here because the time is right to sell this kind of home."

There was scratching at Gwen's door, and she swung herself out of bed to open it just enough to let Larry wander in. Smiling, she ruffled his fur. "Hey, Larry, are you ready for today? Where's Tom?"

Gwen threw on a white terry robe as she followed Larry out the door, waving sleepily to the Curtins and Ricky Montbank. They were seated at the table in front of what used to be the solar window. Ricky Montbank had promised to have it replaced before the week was out.

"They're all upstairs getting ready," Mr. Curtin told Gwen as she passed by.

Climbing the stairs to the garden room, Gwen found Niki, Brock, Hector, Carlos, and Tom filling baskets with fruits and vegetables from the garden room. "Nice of you to get up," Hector teased. "Thanks."

"You're welcome," Gwen replied, poking him playfully. She found Tom across the garden room and waved to him. He smiled at her warmly as he returned the gesture.

"Go have your breakfast and then we need help carrying these baskets out. We have a guy coming at nine with a bunch of horses," Tom told her.

"No kidding?" Gwen asked.

"Yeah," Niki said, wiping her glasses on her sweater. "He has horses that can pull wagons, and we're going to load them up with the food."

"How are they getting around the trees?" Brock asked.

"He knows a dirt road around the back way up," Niki explained.

"Okay, I'm going to grab a bite and come right back," Gwen told them. "Be right back."

Gwen pulled her bicycle alongside Tom's as they rode into Marietta. Brock and Niki were ahead of them. They were all riding new bicycles donated by Ricky Montbank's company, as were the nearly sixty or so other residents of Sage Valley, most of whom were also participants in Mary Curtin's effort, underwritten by a grant from Whippersnapper, to make Sage Valley a completely energy self-sufficient town. Once spring came, there would be a program of local farming as well.

This, ultimately, was how they would survive. Even if there was gas to be had, it would only be had by the very rich or the very powerful. The police would need it and the army would need it. People like Gwen and Tom weren't going to be on that priority list. And until the area started using wind power or nuclear power or some other kind of power to fuel electricity, there were going to be some hard times. The town — and its citizens — would never be connected to the world in the same way again.

"Wow. Marietta is a wreck," Gwen commented to Tom.

Tom nodded, gazing around at the closed, boarded-up stores, the abandoned cars, the trash in the streets. In his bike basket were some of the toiletries he and Gwen had picked up during their last trip down the river: shampoo, toothpaste, toilet tissue, razors, and so on.

Beside him, a horse sputtered, causing him to startle. As it drew ahead, its open cart filled with baskets of produce, Hector, who was seated in back, waved to them. "I feel like a pioneer traveling west," he said.

"We *are* pioneers traveling west," Gwen pointed out. It was exactly how she saw them, as pioneers.

The procession stopped at an abandoned gas station, the one people had flocked to just a month earlier, the one with the private fuel tanker.

The crowd quieted to hear Mary Curtin yell out, "Start setting up your stands around this gas station. Remember, we're not taking any money for this. It's a gesture of goodwill. Be sure everyone gets a flyer telling them about our energy workshops and programs in town."

"What if no one comes out?" a man on a bike asked.

"They'll come," Mr. Curtin said. "They're still hurting for food and supplies."

With a roar, Luke and his pals made a grand show of riding in with the Sage Valley group.

"Listen to this," Gwen said to Tom. "Luke knows the guy who refitted your truck for ethanol, and they're teaching a workshop on how to do it together down at Ghost Motorcycle. Can you believe it?"

"Yeah?" Tom asked, interested. "I learned a lot when I converted my truck. Do you think they might want some help teaching it?"

"You'd want to do that?" Gwen asked.

"I think so."

Gwen smiled at him. Looking around, she noticed that people from

Marietta had already realized what was going on and were streaming into the gas station area, helping the volunteers from Sage Valley to set up their food and supply stands.

A small fireball of happiness and new hope began to spin down at Gwen's very center and it grew stronger and brighter by the moment, until it felt like it filled her. Maybe the world didn't have to be a pit of greed and overconsumption; maybe something better—something like what was happening right then and there—was really possible after all.

It was true—the world had ended. And now the new world was beginning.